## MCCULLOUGH'S JAMBOREE BOOK 2

# KATHI S. BARTON

This is a work of fiction. Names, characters, places, and incidents are products of the author's imagination or are used fictitiously and are not to be construed as real. Any resemblance to actual events, locations, organizations, or persons, living or dead, is entirely coincidental.

**World Castle Publishing, LLC**
Pensacola, Florida
Copyright © Kathi S. Barton 2016
Paperback ISBN: 9781629895598
eBook ISBN: 9781629895604
First Edition World Castle Publishing, LLC, October 3, 2016
http://www.worldcastlepublishing.com
Cover: Karen Fuller
Editor: Maxine Bringenberg

# CHAPTER 1

Parker walked around the big semi three times before he made his way to the driver's door again. He glanced over at his dad when he came around the back end of the thing, having just jumped down off the hitch. He was glad now that Dad had come with him today.

"Don't see nothing to indicate that it's broke down." Parker said he didn't either. "Strange thing though, like you said, there ain't no scent on it. Like it just appeared here without a driver. Mighty weird."

"No kidding. I saw it two days ago but thought whatever was going on, they'd have come back for it by now. But nothing. And the door is unlocked." His dad asked him if he'd been inside. "Yes. Just to look but not enter. There isn't anything in there either. Like you said, it magically appeared." Parker pulled out his phone.

"You calling the cops?" Before he could tell his dad he was, something came out of nowhere and knocked him on his ass. His dad was backing from him and whatever it was that had attacked. His phone had been tossed away from him, and just as he was reaching for it, a boy appeared. "Christ love a waddling whale."

Parker glanced at his dad, wondering not for the first time where the hell he got his little sayings. But he also knew that he'd been frightened too. The boy picked up his phone but didn't hand it to him.

"I'd rather you didn't bother with the police. They have a tendency to make matters worse for us. And for the moment, she's happy." Parker asked him who. "Reese. We've been on the run for a long time and she's having fun and relaxing. She needs it more than I thought she did. It's been a while since she's been able to do that, relax I mean. And we need the money, I'm afraid. The rig, it's very hard on gas and she's not getting much in the way of work. More than likely due to the men chasing after us."

"I see." The boy looked at his Parker's dad then put out his hand to help Parker up, but Parker ignored it for now. "This woman, she owns this rig? And if so, why is it on my property?"

"It was the only place we could find so that the men trying to find us didn't see it. We won't be here much longer, really. The trees will be turning soon, what with autumn coming. It'll be more visible then and we can't stay. You understand." Parker looked at the hand still offered, then at the boy. "My name is Josh Savage. The Josh part is what I picked out, but the last is what I was given at the lab."

"Lab?" Josh nodded, shaking his hand at him as if to say, take it. "I'm a bit heavier than I look. If you would just back up a bit, I could get up and we can figure out what we're going to do about these men chasing you."

"That would be nice, but it's doubtful that you could help us much. They're very determined, you see." When he put his hand closer, Parker took it. The grip was startling, but it was the immediate connection that shocked him more. The kid was an elite shifter. "I'm not what you think. You're a jaguar, correct?"

"Yes. Parker McCullough. This is my dad, Rich." The boy shook his hand then turned to do the same to his dad. He knew the moment that his dad felt the connection as well. "These people, can you tell me why they're chasing after you?"

"Yes. I can." But when no more was forthcoming, Parker looked at his dad for help. The boy laughed a little. Parker had no idea, but he thought it sounded sort of sad. "I can tell you but alas, I cannot. Reese, she says that I'm too trusting. I suppose in a way that I am. But since I have all the information I need to know about you and that you're trustworthy, I feel I can. But I need to ask her first. She is not trusting at all."

"This Reese…is she in trouble too?" Josh nodded. "And these people that are looking for the two of you, do you suppose they'll kill you when they find you?"

"Not me. Not right away. They need to take me apart, so to speak. To see what I can do if they use their weapons on me. And if I can be made into a weapon. Which, I assure you, I can. But Reese will die. Immediately if they can work it. She is of no use to them other than to get me to do as they wish." Parker asked him if he would do that if they had Reese. "I would like to, but she has made me promise that I will not fall prey to their demands. She said that they would do as they pleased with her even after they capture me anyway, and that if I can, I am to take them all out."

Parker wasn't sure what to do now. If he called the police, which he knew that he should, then he'd have both their deaths on his head. He had no doubt whatsoever that Josh was telling him the truth in this. He looked at his dad when he started to laugh.

"I'm telling you right now that I think this is gonna end badly. Not for you boys, but for those that are chasing that girl and this one." Parker asked him how he'd come to that conclusion. "I don't really know, but I have a feeling now that we're involved — and we were the second that truck there pulled onto your land — that the rest of us is gonna be working on this. I don't know how, like I said, but there you go."

Parker turned to Josh. The kid was smiling at his dad but not saying anything. He didn't know why, but Parker had a feeling the kid didn't say much of anything unless asked directly. Parker looked at the semi again and thought of someone finding it.

"I have a barn we can have Reese pull this into. It'll be safer than it is out here. Also, I don't know where you're staying, with her or not, but I have plenty of room at my place that'll be safer than the truck or wherever you are hiding now." Josh told him. "Then I'm sure of it. Margaret runs a nice place but it's not terribly secure. If she doesn't want to stay at my house, I have a married brother that can put the two of you up as well."

At least he hoped so. And with these guys coming around, it would be a good thing to have them close to Lauren. She was way more bad assed than any person that he'd ever met. Parker looked at his dad when he cleared his throat.

"Might want to go and see this girl. Just to let her know in person what you have in mind." He nodded. "And Parker, I'd make this a request, not a demand. Things don't go well when you boys make demands on women."

"No, I'd never do that. I do think that the semi going into the barn would be better. But if she has other plans that's fine too." He looked at Josh then. "You know where she is?"

"Working. She works for May Roy, at Roy's Place. Reese cooks for the morning group and sometimes, a lot lately, for the lunch one too. They like her." His dad laughed. "You've tasted her food?"

"I believe that I have. Every morning, as a matter of fact. She's been there about a week and a half now, correct?" Josh nodded and smiled. "Thought so. May is a wonderful woman and the best bartender you might want to come across. And Margaret is about the sweetest, most ornery woman you'd want to meet. But neither of them could cook a meal and have it come out right if their lives depended on it. Yes, sir, Reese is a fine cook."

They made their way to his dad's truck. They'd come out here together to have a look at the tomatoes and corn that he'd planted. His dad wanted to open up a little roadside place to get rid of the stuff he didn't need, and Parker had brought him out to show him just how much there was. As he put a bushel of tomatoes and corn with some potatoes in the back of the truck, he thought of the young boy.

He wasn't human, that much was certain. And he'd told him that he wasn't right in thinking he was an elite shifter either. Parker had no idea what that might mean, nor the part about the lab that he talked about. Why a bunch of men would want anything to do with this kid was beyond him; especially enough to kill for him.

As they loaded into the truck, Josh telling him that he'd meet them there, he watched as he flew away as a beautiful red tailed hawk. His dad said his name quietly as he backed out of the field.

"Look." They both turned to see a black SUV go by them. It was going pretty fast so he doubted that anyone in the thing had seen the truck, but he worried. "I'm thinking we might want to circle our wagons. There is gonna be trouble if we don't help them."

"I agree." As he reached for his family, he was glad when Lauren said she was in town and would go by the diner to look around. He told her about the boy and the woman; also about the semi that was parked on his land.

*I'll see what I can do about that too. Bear is with me, as well as a few others. We're here looking around for someplace to have a couple of meets and greets.* He was almost afraid to ask her what that meant. *I'll keep an eye on things on this end for you. And Bear is gonna move the vehicle now. The barn unlocked?*

*Yes.* He didn't ask how Bear was going to move the big rig. There had been no keys in the sucker that he'd seen, and he was pretty sure that, without her knowing them, Reese wasn't going to hand over the keys to them. *Just tell him not to damage anything on the truck or the barn. I have stuff in there for the house that I bought cheap, but I don't want it damaged.*

She was still laughing at him when they pulled up in front of the diner alongside three big black vehicles without any sign of license plates. He could see the men in the cars as he walked by them. Parker felt the hair on his neck dance in fear.

~~~

Reese nearly screamed when someone spoke to her from behind. When she turned, holding the spatula like a weapon, the woman simply took it from her and pointed to the walk-in. Reese started to ask her what the hell she was doing when Josh came in the back room with them.

*She's going to help us.* Reese wanted to ask him how and why they might need help when he continued. *They're here. And before you think to run, they're all around this place. Do as she asks, please. I think she can help us.*

She was so afraid that she stood there for a few seconds

just staring at the woman. When the woman pulled out a gun and then nodded to the walk-in again, Reese went where she was told, grabbing Josh's hand as she passed him to take him with her. As soon as the door closed behind them, she looked at her friend.

"What the hell is going on?" He smiled at her but she could see the fear. "How did they find us? We.... The truck. They found the truck, didn't they?"

"Not that I'm aware of. But a man did find it. He said that he'd take care that it was safe." She asked him how they were going to do that. "He has a barn. I have been over his property. The barn is sufficient to hide it in. Also, he said that we should stay with him rather than the hotel. I think that might be a better plan. When I came here, they were at the hotel too. May, she was calling the police even as they left her office."

When the door opened, she had to put her hand over her mouth to keep from screaming. The elderly man standing there smiled at her and asked her to please come with him. Josh started forward and she grabbed him by the arm.

"I don't know you and I'm not going anywhere with you. That woman out there, she has a gun. While I think that can be a good thing, as I said, I don't know you." He nodded and told her that he knew Josh. "How do you know him? Did you call these guys? Did you tell them that I would give him up? I have news for you, you overgrown fucking bastard, I will not go down easily."

"Good for you. And my family isn't going to let a thing happen to either of you now." She started to ask him why but she wasn't given the chance. "Lauren is talking to those men now. She would like for you two to come to the house with me. She assures me that they'll not know you're there. And I'd

11

believe her if I were you. She's got a way about her that makes grown men sob when she doesn't get her way. I love her to death, you see, but she scares the bejeebes out of me too."

"Sob? What the hell is a bejeebe? Never mind, I don't want to know." He nodded and that was when she heard talking. Well, shouting might have been a better term. As she made her way out of the walk-in with Josh, she peeked into the dining room where she knew the woman had gone.

Reese could see her back to her and four men down on their knees in front of Lauren. Two men were standing behind the men, one of them with a gun to the bigger guy's head and the other man holding a knife to the throat of the last guy. Reese wondered what the hell was going on when the woman spoke.

"You see, I don't really give a fucking good shit what you think you're going to have done to me. In the event that you might have missed this, I'm holding all the cards right now." A man spoke then, telling the woman that she was going to pay for this. "Nah, I don't think so. You can think that all you want, but the only thing I might have to pay for is the mess in this dining room should I have to kill you all. Margaret gets kinda pissy when I make a bloody mess in here. She might even bar me from coming here again. It was pretty messy the last time."

Margaret huffed and pushed her ample bosom up when she moved to stand behind the woman. She was a large woman, both the sisters were, but Reese thought that the younger, smaller woman looked meaner by a lot.

"Honey, if you break one table in taking care of these fools, I'll be happy as lemonade on a warm day. They done went and dicked around with our hotel too. Messed up two of the rooms like they owned them. May and me are not gonna be able to rent them out for a time now, and that's just not right. You have to kill 'em, then you go on ahead and do it." The woman asked the men if that was true. But Margaret answered for them. "You darned right it's true. The guest staying there isn't gonna be a bit happy to find all her things a mess."

Her things? Reese wanted to know, but the man behind her touched her arm. When she turned to him, she could see fear and something more. Something in his eyes told her that he was afraid for her. When she shook her head at him, turning back to the scene in front of her, Reese had a feeling that the four men weren't going to get out of there without some heavy fines.

"We're not paying for shit." The man behind him popped him in the back of the head with his gun. "You fucking do that again and I'm going to tear you apart. I'm here on official business. That woman, the one that we were telling you about, she's kidnapped my boss's son. And he wants him back. You either hand him over, with the woman, or I'm going to call in the troops."

"Troops? Would that be the army? Or perhaps you might have been thinking of some other branch of the services?" The man told the woman that he'd call who was necessary to finish this peacefully. "I think that boat has done sank, don't you? Peaceful went out the door the moment you came into my town and messed with my friends. Perhaps later, if you're still breathing that is, I can show you the meaning of the word. I think there might be a dictionary around I can use. By the way, you can read, can't you?"

"Yes, I can fucking read, you cunt. You're going to regret this." She nodded and pulled out her phone. When whoever on the other end answered, the woman said her name, Lauren

McCullough, and that she had a problem here. "You think this is gonna win you points with the boss? I got news for you, bitch, he'll take you down with that brat and woman."

"You think? Here, *my boss* wants a word with you." She held the phone to his ear and when the man paled, Reese looked at Josh when he laughed. When the woman turned and winked at them, Reese backed from the scene. Something was going on there, something bigger than her and Josh.

As they made their way out the back of the diner, she tried to tell herself that this was going to work out. That the woman in there, whatever boss she had, was going to give her enough time to get out of town with Josh. She had no idea how that was going to happen, but she was going to do it. Then the older man said her name and she looked at him. He did look sad.

"You have nothing left at the hotel, child. Those men destroyed everything in the room. Parker is there now with the police getting things squared away. Also, we've had your truck moved to the barn on his place so nobody will notice it. You have to know that you can't keep doing this, running like this. Not now." She nodded. Reese didn't even have the strength to cry. "You come on home with me and we'll have my wife make you up a nice dinner and gather you up something more to wear. Parker will be along in a bit and you can go out to his place to stay. He's a good boy, my Parker."

"They're going to figure out where we are and come there too. You might be better off just dropping me off at my truck. Josh and I need to head out of town now while the getting is good." The man turned the opposite way of her truck and she just sat there. It wasn't until Josh took her hand and reminded her that the truck was hidden in Parker's barn that she started to cry. "We've had a good run, haven't we? I'm sorry. So sorry about this."

"Now you see here. This isn't done. It might look like the storm has come in and is raining on your party, but those men, they don't know what they've messed with in coming to the McCullough doorstep." She nodded at the older man. "Chin up there, child. You're in good hands now. We'll get the two of you safe."

"You have no idea how long we've been running. And what sort of monsters they are. They just don't care who they hurt to get us. Josh is all I have." When Josh said he had to go, she simply rolled down the window and watched him fly away. If the man was shocked, he didn't say anything. Then something occurred to her. "You spoke to Josh. He told you what was going on, didn't he?"

"No. Well, yes and no. We talked to him. My son, Parker, the one that's out there getting things squared away with May, he and I were out looking at the truck you left here. Josh sort of just come out of nowhere at us. Told us a little, that you and him were in trouble, but not why or with who." She said nothing, not sure how much the man really did know. "So when he told us about the diner, we were headed out that way when those cars flew by us. Josh, he went on ahead to see to you and we come in a little later. My daughter-in-law — that's Lauren that came in with me — she was already in town with her men and headed in first. She's scary, that one is. Love her to death, but she can be a mite intense when she's got herself in a pickle."

"Yeah, I noticed that too. But we're broke and down on our luck. I was doing okay for a while, then the runs sort of dried up for us." He nodded but didn't question the way of her runs. "Josh isn't really my nephew. He's my friend."

"Didn't figure that after meeting you. I know that you're

human and he...well, he ain't. I can see that the two of you are close though. Yes, ma'am. He sure does love you." She told the man that she loved Josh as well. "My name is Rich McCullough. My missus, Bea, she's rounding you and the boy up a meal right now. It might be a little cramped at the table with us all, but you just leave that to us. We'll get you in."

"You don't have to do this, Mr. McCullough. We'll be fine once we're rolling." He only told her that she was all right. "I don't want these men coming here and hurting you guys. It's our fight."

"It's mine too, and that of my family. When you parked on the land out there, you sort of give us the okay to take you in. You're not going to be with a better family than this one." She didn't say anything, knowing that talk was cheap and she was going to be going as soon as she could get Josh to her. "Josh mentioned a lab, said that's where the men are coming from. You work there?"

"No, I never worked there. I did deliver things to there for a time, but I never worked there. And after talking with Josh, I'm glad that I never did." She waited for him to ask her about Josh but he only nodded. "Those men aren't going to give up. They want him back. And as I said, they'll go to great lengths to get him."

"Well, I'm not worried and you shouldn't be either. It's not going to happen. Not so long as you're here with us." Reese said nothing again. "I'm assuming that Reese is your right name. May called you Anna. Anna Reese. You thinking that was gonna hide you some?"

"I wasn't sure. I've never been on the run before." Mr. McCullough laughed and said he'd not been either. "I think you should just let this go. As I said, these men aren't going to give up, and they'll hurt or kill whoever is in their way."

"You just leave them to us. We'll take care of them." She thought of all the things these men, all of them, had done to people who had helped her. Reese knew that she shouldn't have stopped to work for the little diner, nor stayed in the small but clean hotel, but she'd been tired and broke. She would have to take better care from now on. "What's the name of this here lab?"

"Barker Benton Institute of Regeneration. It goes by BBIR." She looked at the man when she told him the name. It hadn't been her intention to tell him. In fact, she'd not told a single person she had asked for help what the name was. "You made me tell you."

"No. I'd like to think I had that much power over someone, but I didn't. And so you know, I'd not do that to you anyway. You're worn down and that just slipped out. You'll see, we're a good group of people to have in your corner. Lauren, she's going to have a look-see into them and find out what she can. Her and my son, Colin, they'll have a whole lot of information before dinner is done, I'm betting. And a way to figure this out too. We got us some pretty powerful people in our neck of the woods now, you wait and see."

"You mean Lauren's boss?" He looked at her and nodded. "I'm betting that he's just another man with a lot of money just waiting to get Josh in his hands. Well, I got news for everyone…over my dead body will he ever go back there and be tested on."

"I believe you. But when Lauren and Colin sit down with you to talk about this, I'd like for you to have an open mind. Her boss might just surprise you." Reese doubted it. She had become really jaded over the years on the run. "Here we go. Home sweet home."

# Chapter 2

Parker stretched his neck until it popped twice. He wasn't in the best of humors right now, and the fact that the man in front of him thought it was funny that Parker called the police in pissed him off more. There was so much damage done to the two rooms in the little hotel that he was sure that it was going to cost Margaret and May more than they got in rent for an entire year to have it fixed up. He decided that he'd help them out if they'd let him.

"You really think that we didn't anticipate having a little trouble with the law? Boy, you have no idea who you're fucking with on this." He didn't but he had a feeling that he was going to find out soon enough. As the cruiser pulled into the parking lot, an hour after he'd called them, he wanted to hit someone. And his mood did not improve when his brother pulled in right behind him. Colin, he thought, looked too fresh and in too good a mood to have gotten far with the other place. "You'll see soon enough how money can make things work out for us."

"Hello, Parker. You having some trouble here?" He

wanted to shift, leap at his brother's throat, then go kill the others. "You should know that I can see your cat. And that's not helping matters."

"I'm not having a good time here. This fucking bastard has outright claimed that he's paid off some people, and think it's fucking all right to tear up someone else's property and to take whatever they fucking want." He stretched his neck and felt it popping again. "They're claiming that this woman, whoever the fuck she is, has kidnapped a kid and is now running with him."

"What woman?" Colin looked at him and winked before looking back at the men on their knees. "What woman has kidnapped what person? And before you answer that, neither room here had a woman and child in it."

"Yes, there was. I can see the shit she left lying around, and that's for sure a woman. Unless it belongs to you two. Is that it? And that *woman*, she lets him do whatever he wants." Colin asked how that was kidnapping. "Because he doesn't belong to her, you fucking moron. He's ours."

"Ours? You mean all of you have fathered this child?" Colin looked back at him. "Christ, the things you learn from people nowadays. Five men have fathered one—"

"Don't be obtuse. I said he belonged to us, not that we were his fathers. I swear to Christ, you two are going to regret this as sure as shit." The man stood up, only to be shoved back down by one of the officers. "Get your fucking hands off me and let me go. Do you have any idea how much shit you're bringing down on your own heads with this?"

"You keep saying that. As if we're supposed to be shaking in our boots. I'm not, just so you know. But maybe you should tell us. Who is it we need to be worried enough about to be scared of?" Colin was busy questioning the man when Parker saw Lauren a few seconds before she stood behind the group of men. When Colin turned and looked at her, Parker could almost feel the love between these two. "Ah, there she is. The woman of the hour."

The man who had done all the talking up until now stood up. But when he saw Lauren, he turned his back on her. It was a bad move, made more so by the fact that she was already looking pissed off. The moment the man was opening his mouth to talk to them again, she had her gun at the back of his head and his arm pushed tightly up behind his back. When told to go down, the man did so without a word.

"I've had about enough of your shit, and that of the men you came with." The man asked her what she thought she was doing. "At the moment, I'm playing nicely. See? I've not shot you in the head as yet. Nor have I made a mess of you to send a message to whoever you work for about what it means to fuck with me and my family. But that's not to say I won't, I just haven't yet. So don't fuck with me...I'm having a hard time thinking of a single good reason not to end all of you. Do you have any fucking idea what sort of shit you've brought down on yourselves today? And it's not even ten o'clock yet. Mother fuck, I have better things to do than babysit a bunch of wannabe's."

"You talk really big for a woman with a gun."

Lauren looked at Parker, then at Colin. There was a look there, one that frankly scared him a great deal. And when the gun was handed to Colin, he and Parker stepped back. Parker had a feeling the man had just made the biggest mistake of his short life.

"You think you can take me on, big boy? I don't think you have the balls. And if you do, you should understand that I've been trained by the best. Then I trained them." The man stood

21

up; facing Lauren again, he took off his jacket. "Ah, so we're going to play? Good. I have to tell you, I'm a little rusty right now. Being married, it's fun, but I don't get to have as much activity kicking ass as I used to. Unless you count sex. And wow, that is a very active sport when done correctly."

"When I beat you to shit and piss on your head, what happens to me? You gonna say I abused you? Then have these pieces of shit take me in some place and I'm never heard from again? Boo hoo, the little girl had her nails broken. You're so going down, bitch, you just don't understand how far." His voice had taken on a whiney tone when talking about her nails, like he was mocking Lauren, which Parker was pretty sure he was. Another mistake for this bozo. "I tell you what… you just concede that as a man I'm able to win this, and I'll go about my way and look for this broad."

"Broad? Oh, the woman you claim has kidnapped a little girl. Oh goody. He's going to let me get off with just a warning." The man corrected her, saying it was a boy not a girl. Lauren handed he and Colin a knife, another gun, as well as a handful of items he wasn't sure how she might have used. There were also five extra clips for the gun, which she took from various places on her body, as well as a long piece of wire. She turned back to the man. "Let's just for a moment say I win. What is it you're going to give me? And no, the cops here won't help you when you cry like a little baby."

"Funny. What do you want? And before you answer that, you're not going to win, so you might as well shoot for the moon, bitch." Colin didn't look happy. Hell, Parker wasn't either. But Lauren, they could both tell, was having a good time. "Come on now. I'm betting you want to get your nails done. Or a shopping spree. How about—?"

Her fist hit him square in the face. Not a girly hit either;

she bloodied his nose, lips, as well as his chin. And when he lifted his hands up to hit her, Lauren hit him a second then a third time in quick hard pops. As he staggered back from her blows, she kicked him in the belly, the groin, as well as his knee. The man dropped, his body curled into a ball while she stood over him. When she started to undo her pants, it was Colin that stopped her. Christ, Parker thought, she was going to piss on him.

But the fight had been fought and Lauren had come out the winner. Again. Had he not been standing there, Parker would have missed the entire thing, it had been that fast. When she looked at her nails and laughed, Parker smiled as well. One thing about Lauren, he'd learned over the last few weeks, she did not suffer fools well.

"You did make me break a nail. Damn it. Now I have to find my little knife and file it down again." Then she turned to the other men who had not moved an inch since she challenged their boss to a fight. "Any of you want to take over where he left off? I have to tell you, I'm getting my feet under me now. I could easily take you all three on at once should you like."

Not only did they shake their heads no, but two of them moved out of her reach, just in case, Parker thought. Laughing as their boss was loaded up on a gurney and taken to the hospital by ambulance, Parker stood in front of the remaining men.

"Why are you here?" One was a shifter and the other three were human. The shifter, one of the men who hadn't tried to get away from Lauren, glared at him. "You can tell me now or I bring in someone that you'll have to tell. She's old, mean when she's been woke from her sleep, and can rip your head off without a second thought. Then she might drain you dry or let you bleed out right here on the ground. Either way, you're going to tell me. Or do I call her in?"

"We work for a man that is way scarier than this vamp will be. Trust me when I tell you that." Parker looked at Lauren, who just shrugged. "Kill me now. If you don't, he will when we return to him empty handed."

"All right." The gun exploded before he could realize what Lauren was going to do. Parker stared at her. "What? He said he was going to die anyway. I'm willing to kill the other two should you need—"

"His name is Fritz Henderson. He is the head of the lab department at the Barker Benton Institute for Regeneration. I think they do cell replacement or something like that." Parker said nothing as man number two continued. "About four years ago they put out that there was this kid that had gotten away from the lab. Nobody ever said what he was doing there. We all figured it was some kid of one of the workers. The story we got just didn't jibe with the things we found out about the kid, but we went with it. The money was just too good to pass up. Then about a year ago, we were told that some woman had him. We were to capture and bring them both to the lab."

"This Henderson guy, do you know where he might live?" The man told him that he had no idea, he'd never spoken to him; Don Stafford had. "Which one of these idiots is that? The one that was beaten to shit?"

"No. That guy, the one with the big mouth that thought he could take on that woman and come out on top, would be my report to, David Shoe. Stafford had us come here when he heard that she was working at some diner. Said that we were to find whatever we could in the hotel room, then make it so that it would look like a robbery or something." Parker asked why it took four men to do that. "We were told that the boy was going to be here. We got this memo telling us he was dangerous. I'm not sure how that works, but I guess Stafford had some dealings with him and he knew first hand that he was dangerous. We were told that he hung around in the rooms until the girl returned. But when we got here and the kid wasn't there, David went a little shit crazy and messed up the rooms."

Parker didn't know what else to ask him. The names alone were more than he'd thought they'd get. He looked at Lauren and Colin. Surely one of them would know what the fuck was going on.

"Did it ever occur to you that this isn't a kidnapping and that the kid decided to escape whatever was going on there?" The man nodded at Colin. "And this kid and woman, what makes you think that they're together? Or for that matter, why the hell would this Henderson person want them back when it's obvious that they don't want to be there? You'd better come up with a good reason why this woman and boy need to go back to this lab."

"She was never there. I mean, not a patient of the place. I think somebody said something about her delivering shit, but I never heard what it was." He looked up at Lauren then. "You gonna shoot me too?"

"Nah. You did all right, but that doesn't mean that I won't later. And don't think you're out of the woods just yet. You're going to be spending some time in the local." The man that she'd shot moved, and everyone, him included, looked at Lauren when she laughed. "I only hit him, I didn't kill him. But thanks for making my day in thinking I did. You have no idea how great that makes me feel."

Parker watched as the remaining men were loaded into cruisers. Each of them were fighting to tell something, anything they could think of apparently, to get Henderson caught.

25

Parker wondered if it was because of Lauren, that they were more afraid of her than their boss now. He could understand that, he supposed. Now that they'd spilled the beans, they needed a place to lay low. Parker wondered what the fuck he and his family were going to do now. These people were coming no matter how many questions they got answered.

"We're going to go to the house and have a little talk with our girl. I don't know where the kid is…Dad said he flew off." Parker told Colin what Josh had said to them, about how he wasn't what they thought he was. "That's more than we had before, I guess. Hopefully someone somewhere can dig up something on this Henderson person and why he wants them."

Parker hoped so as well. Right now he had crops to bring in, horses that would need feeding if his hands hadn't done it already, and a big fucking truck somewhere on his land. He rode back to the house with his brother. Parker had a feeling that the shit was about to hit the fan. He just hoped that he and his family didn't get hit by any of it.

~~~

Reese wasn't hurt in any way, but she let the big doctor check her out. When he winked at her, telling the nice older woman in the room with them that she was fit, Reese moved to sit in the chair instead of the bed she'd been on. Boyd, the doctor, sat down in the other one when the woman, Reese thought her name was Bea, sat as well.

"Dad has been out on the porch hoping your friend would return. He will be all right, won't he?" Reese said nothing. She didn't know these people, and she wasn't going to tell them a thing about her or Josh. "I see. Holding things to the vest, are you? I don't blame you. I'd not be terribly trusting either after all this. Oh, I'm to tell you that your rig has been moved to the barn. No one will ever see it without a warrant or a gun. Neither of which will do them much good as far as I'm concerned."

"Why is that?" Bea just smiled at her. "I don't know what's going on here, but I'd very much like to go now. Those men, whoever they are, they'll come back, and when they do, someone is going to get hurt. I've been dealing with them for four years now, and they aren't the type to get warrants if they need one, and they can use a gun better than most cops. Usually armed better too."

"Josh Savage." Reese looked at Boyd. "My brother, Parker, he said that was the boy's name. And that he prefers a hawk to anything else, he thought."

Reese nodded before she could think this was all wrong. "He can be anything, but he said that a hawk makes him feel like he's free. How did you know that? Have you hurt him? If you have, I will hunt you down, each and every one of you, and make you pay."

"He's fine so far as we know. Like I said, my dad is waiting for him to come here. He knows that you're here, I'm assuming, and that we're trustworthy. He told my brother Parker that. Josh hasn't returned, as my mom just told you, so we have no way of knowing his health. But the men at the hotel and at the restaurant are in jail. Well, two are in the hospital, but they're not going anywhere." She asked him how he knew that. "Because when Lauren says they're not, then they're not. She's sort of scary if you want to know the truth."

"So am I." She wasn't, but she appreciated the man nodding like he believed her. "I'm not going to let anything happen to Josh. He's my friend."

"He told Parker and my dad that you were working at the diner to make some cash. Margaret said that so long as you

want the job is yours. May thinks the world of you as well."
Reese said nothing. She was going to miss working with the
elderly women. They were like a breath of fresh air with just
a little hot pepper in it to take away the sugar. "We can help
you, Reese."

"I've been told that before. But there is always a price
that you'll take, isn't there?" He asked her what she meant.
"Money. I'm sure that there is a number that he'll say and
you'll turn us over. This guy, he has a great deal of it thanks
to the government paying him to do these things. And he
spreads it around like it's his job. Which I guess it is. He'll
eventually figure out what it is you really want, then he'll
offer it up to you with a pretty bow and we're running again."

"But you didn't have a price, did you." Reese looked up
at the man who had just entered the room. Christ, were all
these men as big as fucking houses and look like they could
bench-press a luxury liner? "Josh is in the other room, getting
cleaned up. He had a little fun with a shifter, a wolf in the
yard. Not bad, but they were having fun and his clothing is
torn. The wolf is part of my staff on the ranch."

"If you've hurt him, so help me I'll hurt you more." She
felt the first touch of his voice, calming and full of humor. It
was Josh, and he was all right he told her.

*We can trust these people, Reese. I swear to you, I have looked
and they're nothing but good men and women who do not care
for men harming people.* She had no way of telling him she'd
trusted before, but he seemed to understand. *Parker, the man
you're talking to, he's been helping me in ways you cannot believe.
He found me someone to hang out with. Just as you've suggested I
find too. The wolf that I was having fun with, he's my age and we're
going to run in the woods later today. I like this family. You can
trust them.*

"Josh said that he's all right." Parker nodded but didn't come into the room. "I won't let them take him, nor will I sit here and bring this crap down on you. This is our fight. We don't have much but each other, and I can't stand the fact that someone else might get hurt because of us."

"Not anymore." Lauren came in the room speaking, shoving Parker closer to Reese. "I've done a little digging. It's amazing what you can unearth when you have the right tools. Parker, do sit your ass down. I don't want to have to strain anything talking to you."

"I can't smell you. I doubt any of us can. And we should." Everyone turned to look at her when Parker spoke. "I was in the rig, which should have had your scent on it, but there was nothing. Not at the hotel room either. It's as if you've never been there. Or here. The shifter, before he was taken away today, he said that you were hard to find. Which is wrong if he had your scent. He should have been able to find you anywhere."

"That is because of me." Josh came in the room and sat down beside her. Just to have him there, this close, made her stress level lower a great deal. "I think we need to talk. I mean, we need to talk...you and your family would benefit from listening. There is a great deal going on that you need to be made aware of."

"Josh, we should just go." He looked at her then, sadness in his eyes. She felt tears fill her own eyes as he shook his head. "I can find work somewhere else. There are a lot of jobs out there, and we can do this."

"It's not going to work this time, and you know it." She shook her head at him. "Reese, we've hit the end of our ability to outsmart them. And to outrun them. You know as well as I that they're going to kill us both before this is done. You said

29

yourself that they're getting desperate. And we both know that desperate men make rash decisions."

"I think you're right, Josh. We do need to know everything. But before we start on this, which I'm assuming is going to happen, I'd like to call my boys here." Bea stood up before she could tell her that they were going. Again. "We'll have a lovely dinner and then we'll sit and talk. Like reasonable people about how we're going to kick us some major ass."

"Mom."

All the boys, as she called them, looked at their mother like she'd shocked them. Reese thought it was because of the curse word she'd used, but wasn't sure. The only one that seemed to not curb her language was Lauren. And Reese didn't think many people tried to tell her what to do. When the woman in question turned to look at her, Reese wasn't sure if she should run or just simply roll over.

"I would like a private word with you before the family is gathered. And so you know, they're a bit overwhelming at times." Reese told her she was as well. "Why thank you. Twice in one day someone has complimented me."

"Honey, I don't think either time was a compliment." The big man from the diner turned and looked at her. "My name is Colin McCullough, by the way. This lovely woman here is my wife. She can be a little on the intense side, but we don't hold it against her."

"She's fucking scary." Everyone burst out laughing and Reese felt her face heat up. "I'm sorry. It's been a very stressful few years. But I don't think you should get involved in this. The people chasing us won't consider how nice you are when they put a bullet in your heads."

"They've done that before?" She nodded at Parker. "Well, David isn't talking, but his cohorts are. We should have some information in a few hours. But in the meantime, I think Mom is right, we should have a nice dinner. I'm gonna order pizza's."

"Reese can do that. Cook, I mean." Reese tried to tell Josh to hush. "You should fix them dinner. They'll love it, and you can work off some of your stress. You know how good it makes you feel when you can get a stove under you, as you call it."

"Josh, I'm sure that these people have a perfectly good cook to make their meals. Or if not, I'm sure that Mrs. McCullough can do it." They all groaned in unison. Reese looked at the woman when she smiled at her. "You don't cook."

"Oh, good heavens no. I cannot stand the thought of measuring this or that and mixing it all up. Then to have to figure out what a tsp is over a Tbsp is just makes me ill. The mess alone is too much for me to think about. To be honest with you, I think I'd rather have my husband take me fishing again and me bait his hooks than cook." She smiled again at her. "The cook is off, as a matter of fact, but we do have one. I was going to order out, something that will fill these boys up, but if you want to take a turn at it, then you go right on in. And if there is something that you need or want, then tell me and I'll send them out to get it."

Before she could protest any more, she found herself not just in one of the nicest, most up to date kitchens she'd ever seen, but being shown the large walk in pantry as well as a deep freeze so full that they had to shove more in before slamming the door shut around it. As soon as she filled her arms up with different items from both places, she made her way to the kitchen.

She might not ever get the chance to do this again, so she was going to make it count. Finding cake flour as well as frozen apples, Reese decided on dessert as well. It was time to see if she could remember how to make her grandma's apple cinnamon rolls with pecan caramel topping. Lauren came in just as she was mixing up the batter. Not even her questions were going to ruin her fun.

# CHAPTER 3

Parker was taking the trash out to the cans when his brother Boyd came up to talk to him. He had told him earlier that he wanted to see him, and Parker supposed it was as good as time as ever. When he leaned against the barn where the cans were, Parker asked him if he was all right.

"Yes. I wanted to tell you before the others what I know about Barker and Benton. What I heard they do there." Parker nodded, not sure now that he wanted to know. "They're working on a super combination of paranormals. They're trying to create a machine, someone that can live forever, heal quickly, and can shift into things that we're better off not knowing about. And they want to sell to the highest bidder."

"You mean, something like Josh is? Are you saying that he's a part of what they're doing?" Parker's mind tried to shy away from what his brother was telling him. "They're creating more of him. Or they want to and he escaped. So they have no...I'm not sure what they need him for, but I'm betting it's not to congratulate him for turning out so well. And this being, whatever he is, they're going to use an army of them to kill. Is that what you're telling me? Boyd, they can't do that. It's not right. On so many levels. Besides, he's just a kid."

When his brother only stared at him, Parker leaned against the barn too. The kid couldn't have been any more than fifteen years old if that. And he was…well, he was too nice to be considered dangerous, wasn't he? Parker opened and closed his mouth several times before Boyd spoke again.

"About ten years ago there was this big to-do about some branch in the government asking for help and volunteers to help with a specialized project. I heard about it but never thought anything about it. While I was in my last years of my residency there was always some shit going around about how to make some money. Tests being done. Pills to monitor. I never did any of them, but at the hospital, I saw plenty of the aftermath of them." Parker asked him if it was the same lab. "I don't know. I'm looking into it. I have some buddies that are still in that area. But the kids that would come out of there…. Christ, Parker, they really did a number on them. Even the ones that were able to walk away were forever affected by what was done there. Mentally as well as physically. It was bad."

"You're saying that you think Josh is one of the byproducts of some tests. He's…what? A test tube creation? A surrogate was injected with shit to make him? Boyd, I know that I keep saying this, but he's just a kid. Sort of backward. Kind of shy. What makes you think he's a super man?" Boyd looked at the house then back at him. "Tell me."

"He can change into anything." Parker nodded. He'd heard that. "I don't mean any one of a million creations out there. I mean fucking anything. I saw him."

"Saw him what?" Boyd looked at the house and so did Parker. Josh was standing there, just looking at them. "Boyd, what did you see?"

While he watched, Josh changed. Parker was glad for the building behind him, the fence at his right, or he might have fallen. Josh morphed; there was no other way to say it, he morphed into the rocking chair next to him. Then post that held up the roof over his head. He was their dad, their mom. A flower in the little garden that surrounded the porch, and then he changed to a hawk and moved toward them. But in midflight, just as he might have landed in front of them as this incredible bird, he morphed again, and sat on the ground as a midsized cannon. And Parker would bet any amount of money that, if need be, he could fire on them and kill them both.

Josh took his own body back but he didn't get any closer. Parker was glad for it. He wasn't sure that he'd be all right with him too close at the moment. He'd changed into several creatures, several things, in less time than it would have taken for Parker to become his cat and back. Josh didn't look any less nervous than they felt.

"Please don't be frightened of me. I'll never harm anyone here. But as for Reese, I've let her scent go for you all. I believe that with you being cats, it would benefit her if she were to get captured that someone could find her." Parker nodded, not taking his eyes off the young man. "You're afraid of me, aren't you?"

"Yes." He glanced at Boyd when he said nothing. But Parker was afraid and he wanted Josh to know it. "You're not human, I get that, but what you can do, it's really something to see."

"They wanted me to be able to infiltrate any kind of situation. I can speak any language there is, even a few dead ones. I can become anyone...a man they wish to assassinate,

35

someone that they want to get close to someone important." Parker asked him what he was to do once he got there. "Kill them. It was what they wanted of me. So I left. But this time I left for good."

"For good?" Josh nodded. It occurred to him what he was saying. "You'd tried before. To escape from them. And they caught you all the other times."

"Yes. But the day that I hooked up with Reese was the only time I was able to get away completely." Boyd asked him if he thought he'd actually gotten away, even this time. "No. I guess not. But she's been working hard at keeping me safe. I'm not...In the lab, I was in a controlled environment, as you can well imagine. I didn't interact with people, not unless they were wearing body armor or speaking through a mask. My food was brought to me in small containers, each of them labeled with not just what it was but how many calories it had, what preservatives were in each of them. Carbs as well as sugars. Then one of them left their cell phone in my room. I got my first look at what they weren't showing me."

"They didn't hook you up with computers? Are you serious? That's what I would have done." Boyd's face flushed brightly when he realized what he'd said. "What I meant was, if I was inclined to harm someone, I would choose that route."

"The phone was prohibited. All kinds of Internet based items were not permitted in the same room as me. I thought it was because, and as it turned out, rightly so, that way I couldn't manipulate them. I learned that I could easily unlock doors and windows. Mess with the lockdown system." Josh smiled. "I could do that, and more once I figured out how it worked. And once I understood what was going on, not just with me but the entire process, I decided that I'd had enough. Reese was there that day, her semi backed to one of the loading doors, and I changed into my bird and went to her. I knew from the computer that she wasn't with them; untouchable, they called her."

Before Parker could ask him what sort of things he'd found out, Colin yelled from the porch that it was time to talk. And if they hurried, he'd let them have some of the dessert that Reese had made.

Parker figured that he'd hurt Colin for his share in the dessert if it was anything at all like the dinner they'd had. Christ, he could barely move at the end of the meal, and yet he found himself reaching for just one more bite. Over and over as a matter of fact. He was glad, as well as highly disappointed, to see the bowls empty of leftovers. He thought perhaps he might have killed himself had there been anything left by trying to empty them all by himself. That had been the best meal he'd eaten in a very long time.

Homemade noodles and mashed potatoes. Gravy so smooth that it was like eating pure enjoyment. Pecan crusted pork chops with a caramelized onion glaze. Green beans with small spätzle in them. Cornbread pudding like his grandma used to make. Biscuits, she'd told them, for those who didn't want the cake like cornbread that had been sliced into thick chunks with butter on them. He thought of the way the candied carrots had tasted so good that he found himself taking what his mom had left on her plate when she'd been full, and eating them as well. A man could die a very happy one if he had a mate like this to cook for him daily.

The dishes had been loaded into the dishwasher while he'd been in the yard with his brother and Josh. Hawkins was home for a few more days, and even he was moaning about how full he was. Larson was making cups of tea and Dustin was pulling dessert plates from the cabinet when Reese came out of the pantry behind Parker.

Her scent rocked him. She smelled of the dinner they'd had, the sweetness of the caramel sauce. Carrots in brown sugar. But it was the smell that had his cat roaring at him that had Parker reaching for her, the need to touch her nearly taking him to his knees. But as soon as he wrapped his fingers around her arm, she was turning and attacking at the same time.

It was all he could do not to harm her, or to let her harm him as they fell to the floor. He knew in the back of his mind that he'd startled her, had touched without permission. But she was a wild cat. Her fists hit him in the face, ribs, and chin. He only just managed to keep her from biting him by rolling her to her back and grabbing her hands. Parker watched her face and knew the exact moment she realized what she'd done.

"Are you all right?" She nodded but looked away. "Reese, look at me please. I need to see that I didn't hurt you."

"I'm all right. I was just...It's been very tense and I overreacted." He told her she'd done no such thing. "I nearly unmanned you, and I cut your mouth. I think that's the very definition of overreacting."

"You were protecting yourself. I'm glad to know that if someone touches you with ill intent that you can save yourself. Or at the very least, disarm someone." She nodded and he could feel her embarrassment. When someone cleared their throat above him, Parker turned to find Josh looking down at them. He also noticed that everyone was gone but the three of them. "Did you send them all away?"

"Yes. As soon as she turned on you, I had them leave." Parker started to ask him how he'd managed that and decided for now it didn't matter. "Would you like for me to leave as well?"

To his yes, Reese said no. "Please get up off of me. I think I've caused enough damage for one night."

But he didn't want to get off her. In fact, he would have liked to have been alone, in his bed with her beneath him. But he had to explain things first. There were things going on, and not just her being his mate. Parker knew that he needed to hear what was going on so that they could get down to the business of being together.

Parker rolled off her, bringing her body to his as he did so. When she was sitting over him, her legs on either side of his, he held her still when she started to move. Christ, he hurt, he was so fucking hard. Josh left then, as if he was giving them both a moment to work this out. Parker doubted that there was enough time in a day for them to work out being mates.

"He told me that he wasn't hiding your scent any longer." She nodded but didn't move. "Do you know what mates are? How that works?"

"Yes." She rolled her hips over him, his cock stretching more when she moaned. "You're very thick, aren't you? Hard too. I'm going to stop this now. It's not right."

"Yes, I am hard. And you're not making me any less hard or thick by dancing over me this way. I'm not complaining, but I thought you should understand how much I want you right now." When she started to move off him, he tightened his grip on her hips. "What if you were to come for me? Just ride me like this until you cry out with the pleasure of it?"

"What about you?" She moved her hips again; her fingers moved over his chest, over the buttons on his shirt. "I can't believe that I'm doing this. Nor how much I need you. I've never done this before."

Sitting up, he pulled her blouse over her head. Her breasts

were bare, small and tight. When he leaned down, taking the tiny tip into his mouth, he sucked hard, holding her body to his as he did so. Her moan gave him encouragement, so he took as much of her breast into his mouth as he could. Christ, she tasted delicious.

She was riding him harder now, faster too. And when she dug her nails into his back, screaming in his neck, he bit down hard on her breast. He roared out with the taste of her. Her blood, the warmth of it sliding down the back of his throat, was more than he'd hoped for. Parker rolled her to the floor, his body hard for his own release, but he wanted her to enjoy this. Their first time coupling.

"Come again." Her head shook hard, but her body bowed up. As soon as she came again, her hand over her mouth this time, Parker watched her. Saw the need there and when it was fulfilled. That moment, that small moment in time when she was sated before he brought her again and again.

She was beautiful in her release. He brought her twice more, each time commanding her to come when her mouth was telling him she was spent. He reached between then then, his cock hurting from how full it was, his balls aching like he'd been injured. But he pushed his thumb over her clit, hard into her femininity until she came hard enough for her to faint.

Parker rolled into her body a few more times before he too had to lay his head at her breast. He'd just mated and bonded with his mate, who was a complete stranger as well as a fugitive. Laughing a little, he wondered what other surprise he could expect.

~~~

Josh knew that the two of them were having sex, or as close as they could in the kitchen. He'd been angry at first; it was the reason he'd left the big kitchen. But now that he

40

thought of it, how it had worked out for them, he was glad. Reese deserved a man in her life, and he couldn't have picked better for her than Parker McCullough. When Colin asked him where they were, he sent him to his wife. There was no point in rushing this now; the talk was going to happen sometime but not right this moment. When he felt her anger and embarrassment, mostly the latter of the two, he stood up and moved to the kitchen. He wouldn't go in, but he would remind them that people were waiting for them.

"We're coming." Josh only smiled at the frustration in Parker's voice. "We'll be right there. And since you told me that you got everyone out of here earlier, you can damn well make them wait. Please?"

"I can do that. I shall entertain them."

He tried to think of a story, something in his life that had been funny. Or even fun. There wasn't anything, especially not until after he'd met Reese. He decided to tell them that story. The meeting of kindness. When everyone was seated, bursting with sugary confections and their drink, he started out the story just the way it had happened.

"It was Tuesday. In the morning around four. I knew that it was supply day, the day that both food and clean linens were brought to the compound." Boyd asked him how he knew. "Once, a week before, when there had been an accident in my room, I overheard one of the staff say that a truck wouldn't be there for two days. That was on a Sunday."

"Accident?" Josh assured Hawkins he didn't want to know. "But I think we need to know. It will go a long way in us knowing the sort of people that we're going to be dealing with."

This man frightened him. Josh had no idea why, he was as gentle as a puppy he'd seen in yards and on the Internet. But he thought that he could also be deadly when necessary. That at a moment's notice, he could go from just being a regular man and shift into a wild animal that would tear someone part. So he nodded and changed his story to suit the needs of this man. And perhaps the family as well.

"They would draw my blood. Several times a day, as a matter of fact. And one day, the nurse had a hard time entering my vein. And before you ask, yes, I did that. Not that she wasn't sticking me, but she thought that she wasn't. I can do that to most sub-minded people." Larson asked him if he could do it to any of them. Josh looked around the room, touching each of their minds and finding them to be above intelligent, as well as open for him to look should he want. "No. Not to the extent that I could there. I can suggest something, sort of beg for it, but I can't make any of you do anything. Nor can I manipulate Parker or Reese. But the others here, the staff and the other humans around, I can." He was told to go on with the story.

"Reese was at the dock when I flew by the open door. She was being screamed at by one of the men there. A burly man who thought that his weight alone should have gotten him what he wanted. Which, in this case, was Reese. But she was having none of it." He smiled when he thought of how she'd taken on a man three times her size and had nearly beaten him. "When she was injured, her body tossed over the edge of the dock plate and into the back of the empty cargo truck, I shoved the man back with my mind and watched her. When she finally was able to move to the front of her truck, I flew into the open window and changed so that no one would question her why I was there."

He didn't tell them that he'd killed the man. He'd been just what he'd been made for...a killing machine. Nor did he tell them that he'd crushed the man's body against the concrete wall hard enough to crack it, along with his skull. Josh turned to look at the woman who had been dying, her own injuries so bad that he'd had to help her, when Reese and Parker joined them.

"There was no one about, so when she was ready to go, not saying a word to me or asking how I'd gotten there, we pulled off the lot. I was able to keep her safe and unseen until we were well cleared of the place. When I thought us far enough away for her not to return me to my prison, I appeared to her. As I am now." He laughed and looked at Reese when she joined him. "You were frightened."

"You scared me into nearly driving into a bridge." She sat down on the room's only single chair and glared at Parker before looking at Josh again. "You were a clipboard. Something that I used every day on my job; you became one to run away."

To him it was a perfect way to start on some of the things he could do. But when he looked around the room, ready to explain should they want to ask him things, he realized that they were no longer interested in his story but at the couple that had just joined them.

Parker wasn't upset, not that Josh could see. Parker was happy, he thought. Feeling something that few people got to enjoy. The fulfilment of his lives, the other half to himself. A mate, someone to love for all time. But there was trouble brewing too. Josh could see that for all his own happiness, Reese was not.

"She's your mate, son?" Parker nodded at his dad, never taking his eyes off Reese. "Well I'll be hang tied and hung out to dry. You've found her. Welcome to the family —"

"I am not going to be his mate." Mr. McCullough stopped talking and moving toward Reese when she spoke. "Don't

43

you see what kind of mistake this will be? Those people will hurt all of you, especially him if they think they can get to Josh. I can't let that happen to any of you. This is all wrong."

"Wrong or not, you're mated." Josh stood up when he didn't care for the tone that Boyd was using. "I'm not saying that this is going to be easy or without problems. But as of the moment the two of you came together, you became our family; and we do not, under any circumstances, let anyone hurt family. And that would include Josh as well."

"No. I'm not family. I'm not even human." He'd been so surprised by the gently said sentence that he'd backed from the emotions. Boyd was a wonderful man, sincere in what he was saying too. "It's great that Reese has you all, but I have to do this on my own."

Mr. McCullough patted him on the back. "Too late for that, young man. When we induct you into this family, you're not getting away from us. Nor will anyone hurt you, either, so long as we're here to help. And if they do.... Well, they won't have a second chance at it, I'll tell you that right now."

Reese was hugged and welcomed when he was. Parker didn't get any closer to his new mate, but he did keep an eye on her. When Josh made his way to him, Parker smiled at him and Josh was warmed by it. There was something so heartwarming, so wonderfully consuming about having someone look at you like you were a person and not a weapon.

"She's upset with me." Josh asked if Reese was upset with him or herself. "Both, I guess. I tried to explain to her that we're going to work hard at getting this straightened out, but she doesn't believe me."

"She will." They both turned to look at her when Lauren laughed. "You will all need to know the whole of our story, however. It will be painful for the two of us, Reese and I, but I think it's important that you are well aware of what we have gone through."

"I agree. And when we settle here, after they've talked to her, we'll get it taken care of." Josh started back to his seat but Parker said his name. "I'd be honored to have you come and live with us too. I know that you and Reese have been together for a while now, and I'd very much like for you to stay with us."

"I've never lived in a home before." Parker said he was working on his house and it had a way to go as yet, but it was a home he loved. "You have much on your plate at the moment. But with your family here, I'm sure that they won't allow you to fail, Parker."

Parker glanced at Reese before answering Josh. "I hope so." So did Josh. "But in the meantime, you come and stay with us, and maybe we can get a room or two finished before the shit hits the fan."

Josh nodded, thinking it an apt description of what was coming. The men at the lab wouldn't give up, he knew this. What he worried about more was just what Reese was concerned about. The McCullough jamboree might be hurt, yet he had a feeling that the lab guys would be dead.

# CHAPTER 4

Fritz watched as his techs monitored the computers. This was the ninth time in as many weeks that they were trying out a mixture of DNA. The mechanical arms in the closed off white room were working just as they should have been, picking up vials and taking out just the right amount, but Fritz was worried. This was getting tedious and expensive. And they were no closer to finding the formula than they had been all those months ago.

SA-8 had been their only success so far. And even in that, it hadn't gone as planned. The thing had had the ability to do so much more than they'd thought it would. Which Fritz supposed was good, but it had hidden it from them until it was too late for them to take advantage of it. The little monster was going to pay for that. Like its ability to think for itself, as well as work the computers. That had been a fatal mistake for a great many people.

"The last of the samples is being added now." Fritz looked in the white room, then at the monitors as he continued to think of the kid. "Once those are added, sir, we should know immediately if it works."

"It had better." He'd not been here when SA-8 had been created. His wife had decided that she needed to get away. From what, he had no idea. She did nothing all day, didn't even lift a finger to pick out her own clothing. But get away they had. And he'd missed his first and only creation being brought into the world.

Fritz had no idea how long it had taken for them to know they had a viable sample. Immediately to these fools could be anything from right now to in a week. And as they'd had none work since, he wasn't sure what he should be watching for. But what he did know that the others didn't was that the woman who had given birth to the boy hadn't been human at all, not really. He wondered if that had been the key ingredient. Fritz thought that might have been the biggest mistake he'd made to date.

She'd been a witch, and a very strong one too, apparently. Once they had taken her to surgery and had performed the necessary operation for her to carry SA-8, she'd gone from an almost docile captive to someone that they all feared. Even him. He'd been so surprised by her feral actions that he'd ordered the staff to stay away from her, and if they could, to find a way to abort the creature that she carried.

So because of their fear of her, no blood work had been performed and no prenatal care had been given to her. They simply could not do anything with or to her. The drugs that they had used on her to put her under prior to that suddenly had no effect on her. Fritz wondered if they had worked at all. Anytime anyone got within a few feet of her cage, she had hurt them. Most would just be rendered unconscious; others that were, on his order, sent to kill her, would be murdered themselves. They'd gotten to the point where they'd just left her alone, only to watch over her via cameras.

She would neither eat nor take water from them once she'd been implanted. He had no idea how she'd lived long enough to carry the child to term, but she had apparently. It wasn't until she'd given birth that they'd been able to go into the room without any trouble. And once the child had been born...well, it was still a mystery where the bitch had disappeared to. They'd found only a swaddled babe in the room five months after it had been conceived.

"It's a fail." Fritz looked at the monitor when the man next to him spoke. "We'll go back and see what was in the last vial and work that around again. I believe we've miscalculated one of the DNA's."

"You *believe* you might have miscalculated? I'm pretty sure that's a given, don't you?" He pointed to the monitor before continuing. "I know that we've gone over this time and time again. But it bears repeating, don't you think? If we do not come up with the correct formula, and soon, we're all going to be out of a job. And there might even be a few more spouses mourning the loss of their loved ones because of it."

"We're trying, sir. I swear to you, we're working all day on this, and into the night." Fritz told him they weren't working enough. "Sir, we have gone over our notes and over them. But without the last pages, we cannot know what we did before. That is the key, as you know."

"Yes. I know. But as we've combed every square inch of this place, torn out walls and emptied trash receptacles; we know that they're not here." Someone had taken them, or they had been destroyed. Which was what he actually thought. "Get me the results that I need or so help me, I'll find someone that will."

As he made his way back to his offices, he pulled out his

cell. The thing didn't work in the labs; he'd taken care of that the moment he'd realized how SA-8 had gotten away. It had taken him another two years, two fucking years, to figure out that he'd had help. And finding that bitch had been harder than he thought.

There were seven missed calls, two of those from his dear wife and one unknown. Ignoring the calls for text messages, he looked through his message system to see who he had to suck up to about money. The one that simply said Ohio had him thinking it was David again. He dialed it first, needing to hear something positive for a change.

"I do hope you have some good news." There was silence at the other end, eerie silence. "David?"

"No, not David. But I do know who you are now, and where. Nice place you got there, Fritz. You should take better care with your security system. It's way too easy to break into." He looked around the hall and then at the camera. "There you are. Hey, you should think about using the gym in the labs there, buddy. You're looking positively fat. And that tie looks like someone climbed up on your shoulders and took a nasty dump. Looks like shit. Get it, looks like.... Never mind. Anyway, you should consider getting out more. You have some major love handles."

"Who is this? And how the hell did you get my number?" The woman laughed; it wasn't forced either, but like she found him to be really funny. "I asked you a question, bitch, and I demand that you answer me. I've got the federal government on my side, and we will find you."

"How the hell do you think I found you? And the government that you think you have on your side? Well, I'd not count on that happening much longer. In fact, I'm verifying that this is your phone before you get the call. I love that, *the call*. Like you're up for some sort of award." The laughter again, then it was cut off abruptly when she spoke again. "Listen up, fuckwad. As soon as we get there, you're going to be not just shut down, but spending a lot of time in federal prison as well. Fucking idiot. Didn't you think someone somewhere would figure out that you're fucking with people's lives?"

"Who the fuck is this?" He didn't expect an answer and didn't get one. "When I find you, you're going to regret this."

"I already do." He made his way to his office, swiping his badge to enter his own domain. "Won't work."

No matter how many times he swiped his card over the reader, nothing happened. The green light that indicated that he had the right barcode didn't light up like it was supposed to. Fritz wondered why he was still on the phone with this woman when she told him that she had control of all his security.

"Let me in my fucking office, cunt, or so help me, I'm going to make you pay." She asked him how he was going to manage that when he couldn't even figure out who she was. Nor get into his own office. "You wait. I have men working for me that will find you."

"David Shoe? I wouldn't count on that. He's being detained. Oh, and Don Stafford, he's singing your praises too. Not in a good way, in the event that you're wondering. I had to knock them around a little…it was fun but short lived. Where do you get your henchmen, Fritzy? Henchmen are Us? I think you get what you pay for. They're not worth fuck if you ask me. But they're giving us all sorts of intel on you. Some I'm betting you didn't know they had. Sort of puts you in a bad way, doesn't it? What with all your men, as you called them, giving you up." Fritz tried to think when the last time was he'd spoken to either man. "There is a lot of shit going on, Fritzy, and you're going to be getting your just desserts too... soon enough."

"Stop calling me that. And who the fuck are you?" Nothing. Not even the laughter this time. But he knew she was still there...he could hear the ambient noises in the background. "When I find you, and I will, you are going to pay for this. Open my fucking door."

The door unlocked then opened. It slid open like someone was there pushing gently on it. He was terrified, really, of using the obvious trap. Fritz hadn't used his badge and he'd not pulled on it. As he peeked in the room, trying to see if he might be ambushed when he did walk in, the woman on the phone laughed again before speaking.

"Thought you'd like to know I've been busy since I found out about you and your cohorts. As of right now, funding has been cut off, mother fucker. Not only that, but in about two minutes, you're going to be raided. You should have left when the getting out was good." He heard the explosion down the hall. "Oops, I think they jumped the gun a little."

He entered his office and shut the door. Throwing the phone across the room, he heard the resounding shatter of glass when it hit the cabinet. Not even bothering with the mess, something he would normally clean up, he went to his safe. Hopefully, whoever this bitch was she'd not gotten into his stash. As soon as it opened, he heard the noise down the hall, shots fired, and people screaming.

Pulling out what he had in there, all of it in a big bag ready for a run, he turned and went to the wall unit where the phone had shattered the glass. Pressing on the handle in the drawer then turning it to the left, he waited impatiently for the wall to slide open. The noise outside his office had him turning just as he entered the darkness of the opening.

*Run,* his mind told him. *Get out.* He found himself debating, wondering if this was a joke. There wasn't any way that the government was going to shut him down. But as soon as he heard the man telling him to open up, Fritz pressed the button to close himself into the hallway and to escape to freedom.

There were noises behind him, he could hear them as he made his way carefully down the dark hall. He knew that no one but him knew about the hidden door. The three men that had helped him put it in were now long dead, their bodies buried deep within the concrete that now housed part of his lab. The second doorway was a little trickier than the first, and it took him a full five minutes of trying to calm himself before he was able to remember the way to do it. As soon as it slid open, he stood in a large bunker-like housing and let out a long breath. He was safe. From what, he had no idea, but he felt better just knowing that he wasn't going to prison.

He knew that he could stay down here for three years. Longer if he could get the garden that was just waiting to be used working. Fritz had never been one to do such tasks, leaving that to the professionals. But he'd gotten books on it, read up on seeds and the needs of making it work. All he had to do now was wait whoever this person was out. And he knew that he could do that easily.

He put his bag on the desk that matched the one in his office above him and sat down. Christ, he was terrified. But safe. He had no idea what was going to happen to the people above him. There had been a time when he had thought of putting in a camera system, just to be able to come here and also monitor above, but he'd put it off, thinking, like a fool, that he was set up for life. That no one would try and shut him down once he was able to produce the monster that they wanted.

After an hour of just wandering around the compound, he finally sat at his desk again. Pulling his bag to him, his life's work, he opened it up. Looking down at the contents, he started to laugh. Then cry. He'd been fucked over, it seemed. By the woman on the phone.

~~~

Parker wasn't sure what to do with himself. He'd never been one to be lazy or idle. But right now he couldn't think of a single place he'd rather be than out in the barn. Or the paddock. Anywhere but in his home trying to figure out the woman and boy with him.

"It's a big house." He looked around the living room, the only room that they'd ventured into since arriving over an hour ago. Parker asked her if she wanted to see the rest of it. "I'm not sure why you think I need to be here with you. You do know that they're going to come for us, right?"

"Yes. You've said that several times since we got here. But we're protected here. The security system on the house is foolproof, and even if someone managed to get close to us, there are any number of pack and jamboree around the yard and woods behind us." Reese nodded as she ran her fingers over the back of the couch. Josh was sitting in the big overstuffed chair that had come with the set and saying nothing. "The kitchen is through here. It needs some work yet. The counters have arrived...well, they've been here for a week or so, but I've not had time to put them in. I do have the floors in. They're heated so they can be warmer in the winter, but that's about the extent of the improvements that I've done."

"You're doing this on your own?" He nodded and told her it was fun. "I can see that. I do a lot of my own repairs on the truck when necessary. It's expensive to have some guy do it. I'd like to see the kitchen, if you don't mind."

"I've had the truck looked over too, by the way. Bear, the friend of Lauren's, said it might have a bug or two on it." She asked him what he meant. "Trackers. But apparently he didn't find any. However, he did find some issues, smaller ones that he enjoyed taking care of. I think he's planning on putting on new tires next. Lauren told me that at one time he worked on the rigs in the service or something. He's misses that."

"He doesn't have to do that. Besides, I really don't have the funds for that." He watched her as she glanced over at Josh before continuing. "We've been on the road for a while now. I've not been...Routes have been getting next to impossible to line up. So as you can imagine, there's not been a lot of extras for us."

"I would imagine that Henderson has had a lot to do with that." She nodded and looked at him. "Come into the kitchen with me. I'd like to have your input on the way things are going. If you want to change things, we still have plenty of time."

She followed him, but he could tell that she wasn't going to have any kind of opinion on the way he had it laid out. Either she didn't want to leave Josh behind, who was now dozing in the big chair, or she didn't want to be alone with him. He thought it might have been both. But mostly him.

"This is what the cabinets are going to look like when I get them all in. But I think maybe I might have over ordered them. I was excited to have a larger kitchen, but I've not been able to do much more than just dream of it until now. I had plans of knocking out this wall, but found out after they were set that it's load bearing." She nodded as she moved around the big cavernous room. "The floor was easy to put down. I wasn't sure I'd like it at first, but once it was laid, I thought it worked well. There is a large fridge here; the built-ins there are done but empty of any food right now. I was waiting on the kitchen to be closer to being able to have a cook in it."

"Why did you want to enlarge this room?" He told her he had a big family and they sort of met in the kitchen when together. "I can see that. Even at your parents' house, most of you would gravitate to that room. Do you have a pantry here?"

Parker showed her the shell that was going to serve as the pantry. It wasn't even walled in yet; he'd been waiting to have the time to put the drywall up that sat in the dining room in a big pile. As he explained to her what he had working, she nodded and made suggestions. The fact that he'd planned to put in a large walk-in refrigerator in his own home made her smile.

"I have noticed that food is a big thing to you guys. I've never seen a group of people eat as much as you do." He told her it was their other halves that helped that along. "Yes. When I was cooking for this restaurant a few years ago, I could almost tell when a shifter or someone like them came in. The appetizers would be huge part of the bill."

"Last night when you cooked for us, you did an amazing job. And that cornbread was a big hit. I think I could have eaten the entire pan of it by myself." She nodded and moved out of the shell to the other part of the kitchen that was a little further along. "Laundry room. There is a second, smaller one on the upper floor that I use when there is a need. I didn't see any point in having to bring my clothing down here to wash, then have to cart them back up. This one is bigger for the rest of the household."

"That's a wonderful idea." He felt her praise all the way

to his toes. When she moved near one of the stacks of tile that he'd had left over and tripped over a piece of equipment he'd left there, he caught her in his arms. "I'm sorry."

"I'm not." He held her, pulling her body to his. "You feel good in my arms. I love the way you fit me."

"I'm afraid this won't work out." She didn't pull away nor did she loosen up, but he'd take what he could get. Asking her why she didn't think it would work, Parker buried his nose in her hair. "Stop that. You're melting me. I don't think this will work out simply because we don't know each other well enough to think it will."

"True. But we have a lifetime to get to know each other. And I'd very much like to get to know you." She turned in his arms and looked up at him. "I don't want you hurt, nor do I want you to think I'm going to hurt you. You're my mate and I love touching you. All of you."

"I know you won't hurt me. I have no idea why I know that, but I do." He thanked her. "Parker, this isn't just about me. This is about the men at the lab, Josh and his safety, as well as your parents and family. These men, they won't stop at anything to get him."

"You've met Lauren, so you know what she is to the government." He lifted her chin up as he spoke, needing to smell her throat. "She's talked to her boss, and they've made plans to go into the lab and shut it down."

She nearly took his head off when she jerked his head up by his hair. The look on her face, the pure terror there, had his cat running along his skin harshly. He asked her what happened.

"They'll get killed." He told her they were good. "Of course they are, but so are the men and women there. I know for a fact that they're armed all the time. Not the lab people, but the rest of them are. They're going to get hurt by going in there."

"Honey, they're already there. They got there about an hour ago." He watched her pace the room. As she spoke, seemingly throwing out ideas and issues and discarding them just as quickly, Parker wondered if he should be taking notes to pass onto Lauren and the rest of his family.

He loved to watch her walk, her body hard with something he didn't understand. Her breasts bounced nicely, her hips swayed to the steps of her feet. But when he noticed that she was facing him, her foot patting the floor like she was pissed, he looked up at her face. "What?"

"Are you finished?" He shook his head and grinned at her. "Well, get over it. I'm not going to sleep with you. So get that right out of your head."

"Oh darling, there will be very little sleep between us when we go to bed. Not that we really need a bed. I could sit you right up here on this makeshift table and take you easily." Her body warmed; he could smell her need, feel it almost. "Do you have any idea how much I'd like to strip you down and take you?"

"No. You don't want that. And neither do I." He moved toward her. Taking his time and letting his cat, never one to simply take no as an answer, run along his skin. He told Parker to take her, to make her theirs, but he told him he had to wait. "You should…I want you to stay back."

"You don't want me?" She nodded, then shook her head. "Which is it, love? Do you or don't you? I want you. With every fiber of my being. And so does my cat."

"Your cat?" She sounded panicky and he nearly laughed. "You can't mean that he wants to have sex with me, do you? I mean, that's just not going to happen. Not ever."

"He wants to taste your cream. Lick your hot wet pussy until you come down his throat. Then fuck you with it, bringing more of your cream into him. The taste of you will be forever his." Reese swallowed hard twice. Parker was close enough to touch her now, so he ran his fingers down her arm to her fingers. "I want you as well. To feel you coming around my cock. Have you screaming out my name when you do so. And then when you're coming, I want to taste you, feel your hot blood as it slides down my throat, filling me with your essence and warmth."

He lifted her up then, cupped her ass and held her to him as he seated her on the empty wiring roll he'd been using. Her fingers ran down the front of his shirt, opening buttons as she went, tearing off the ones that didn't open fast enough. And when he was bared to her, she nipped at his flesh, took his nipple into her mouth and suckled.

Parker held her to him as he pulled at her zipper and button to her pants. His cock ached to take her, to fill her. And when he tore her pants open, no longer able to wait, he tossed them to the floor when she wrapped her legs around his.

When her panties joined her pants, he lifted her again. His cock was at her entrance, his body poised to take what was his. Looking into her eyes, he could see every emotion she was having. Her need was there, front and center. But he could see fear as well. Whether it was of him or the men coming he didn't know, but he watched her.

"You belong to me. None other." She nodded, her eyes closing now. "Say it, Reese. Say that you belong to me, forever."

"I don't want you hurt." He told her he knew that. "This will bind us, forever. We'll be together when these men come. They'll use you to get to me, then to Josh. I can't have any of you hurt over this. They're coming, Parker. And soon."

"I'm counting on that." He watched her face again, seeing her resolve and hoping it was meant for them. "Say it, please."

"I belong to you. Now and forever."

He slid into her, breaking through her virginity at the same time. When she screamed out her pain, he held her to him, holding her tightly while she got used to him, her sheath stretching and rippling along his cock to accommodate his invasion of her body.

Moving to the wall behind her, he pressed her to it, held her while her body stretched for him, strangling and milking his cock. And when she lifted her head from his shoulder, he could see her tears and kissed them away. "I should have told you."

"I knew that you'd never had sex before. I can smell you." He rolled his hips to adjust the stance on his feet. Her body reacted to his, her moan nearly making him take her hard. "I love that you've held yourself for me."

"I didn't exactly hold myself for anyone." She looked up at him and Parker rolled his hips again. "You're making me want you more. I'm sure you know that, but I can't wait to come again."

He took her then, as slowly as he could, rolling his hips so that he wasn't hurting her, rushing her. And when she started to ride him, her hips rolling up and down, he held her so that she could use him as a brace.

"Come for me, Reese. Let me feel you come on me and I'll empty inside of you." Her breath caught then, heated along his neck. Her mouth nipped at his skin, at his neck. When she bit down on his pulse at his throat, not hard but enough to make his body hurt more, he pulled her to him. "Bite me. Now."

Her teeth broke his skin. As he pounded her harder, taking her and him to the highest possible point in their relationship, he tilted her head slightly and bit down on her throat. As soon as her blood filled his mouth, Parker came hard, filling his mate with all that he was.

# Chapter 5

Josh wasn't sure what he was supposed to do in the house. He could have left, he knew that, but he was enjoying the blossoming love between Reese and Parker. Reese was a little shy about what was happening, but Parker acted as if he'd been given every single gift he'd ever wanted all rolled up in Reese. Josh smiled when she came in the kitchen with him.

"I don't know what I'm doing." He just looked up at her. The table from the barn had been brought in last night and put together, and he loved it. "I have to do something. Anything, because when I just sit around I think, and thinking is dangerous. How do you put in cabinets?"

"Excuse me?" When she repeated herself, he looked around the empty kitchen. "I'm not sure. But I'm betting that Mr. McCullough knows. I've never seen a man more informed than he is. Or at least he thinks he is."

"Yes. He's a sweetheart. So is Mrs. McCullough." They'd both been asked to stop calling them Mr. and Mrs. But it had been a hard habit for both of them to break. "Do you think we could do this? I mean, at least figure it out. I can't stand all this clutter, and the fact that we're eating at someone else's house instead of here drives me nuts. For as long as we can be safe, I'd like to be able to cook here."

The office was the only room that was complete. Even Josh's room only had a bed in it with a makeshift closet. He did have a bathroom that was complete, but it lacked anything that was homey. He wasn't upset by the lack of things in the house; he had lived with blank walls and hard floors for most of his life. But he could see where it bothered Reese. As they pulled up videos on how to hang cabinets, he reached out beyond the house to see where Parker was.

The man was a wonder to him. After getting up at the crack of dawn, he'd done more work by eight in the morning than most people did all day. The pigs had been fed, the cows were let out to pasture to graze all they wanted, and now he was out in the fields looking over his wheat. His wheat fields were his pride and joy right now, Josh knew. Parker was planning to grind it come fall and sell it to the local bakeries. Josh hoped that he could be here when that process was started.

"There it is." He looked down at the computer and saw the video. He wasn't sure that just the two of them could accomplish such a thing, but he was willing to try if she was. But after watching it three times, he was glad to see that Reese thought they were in over their heads as well. "Do you suppose Rich would come over and give us a hand? I could bake him a cake or something if we get it done."

"You could promise him that you'd wipe your feet in the grass and he'd be happy to help. I've never seen a man so besotted with someone as he is with you." Josh laughed when Reese blushed. "You could call him. I'm sure that if he thinks he can't do it, then he'll tell you."

"I don't want to be a bother to him." For an answer to that stupid statement, he simply handed her the phone. "All right, but if he says no, then I'm going to blame you."

"All right." Josh watched her. He knew just when Rich said he'd do it. As they made arrangements for him and his missus to come over, Josh reached for Parker again. This time to talk.

*Parker, this is Josh. I'm not sure that you can answer me, but I wanted to make contact with you.* He paused, waiting to see if he'd answer. *I can talk to you, so that's good.*

*I can talk to you as well. But if it's bad news, like, I don't know… something that I don't want to hear, then can you wait until lunch when I'm there? It's been a rough morning so far.* Josh smiled and told him it wasn't bad news. So far as he knew. Then asked him what was going on. *Do you remember me telling you about the mill I was having put in? Well, the plans have just changed. I was hoping for fall, but it looks like it's going to be spring now. Too late for this season.*

*I'm sorry. Was it because of the weather? I know that they've had a great deal of flooding in some areas of the country.* He told him that the buyer had over extended himself and couldn't get to him. *Perhaps this will be better than him making a mistake in trying to get it done sooner. He won't feel as rushed to get it done.*

*I never thought of that. Good job. Now what is it I can do for you?* He told him what was going on. *My dad is good. He and my brother Dustin have been redoing houses for a while now. Make a nice profit of it too. I'm glad that she's getting it done. I might never at the rate I'm going.*

*I think she's needing to get it done so that she can have something to do. She's bored. As am I.* Parker said he was sorry. *Don't be. We're just used to moving all the time, so I think this will do us both some good.*

65

*Let me know if she needs something or doesn't care for whatever I have. I was buying things well before I had the house even started. I think maybe I might have to have a sale when this is over, to get rid of surplus.* They both laughed. *Josh, thank you for her. I know that you and her have been going for a long time, just the two of you. I'm also betting that you've kept her safe too. More than she knows about.*

*I have. But I'd rather her think that she's protecting me. It's easier that way for her. She needed to feel useful, I think, and I needed her companionship.* He'd never admitted to being able to care for himself to anyone before. He was a great deal stronger than even the people back at the lab knew. *You as well, now that you're mated to her.*

*Thank you. More than I can say, I thank you.* Josh told him he would be there if needed. *And me too. Remember, if she needs anything or wants to change it, tell her she can do whatever makes her happy. She certainly has made me happy. And if you're really bored, you can hunt me up on the ranch. I could always use a good partner.*

By the time Rich and Dustin showed up at the house, three more trucks, piled with men and women in them, had as well. No one had gotten out of their vehicles, which confused Josh. Then when Rich waved his hand at them, all at once they emptied out of the trucks and began pouring all over the barn and house. In minutes the cabinets were in the kitchen and walls being taken down in the dining room.

"I've been wanting to do this for darn near a month now." Josh nodded at Rich as they watched several men putting drywall in the pantry. "Parker kept telling me that he had it. Just taking his time. But now that he's got him a mate, he needs to get his home in order. You ever do anything like this before?"

Josh shook his head. "No. I've only been in a lab, then the truck. There aren't that many opportunities to do much in the way of construction when you're on the road as much as we were."

Before he knew it, Josh not only had on a tool belt but was being shown how to use an electric screw driver. Hanging the cabinetry was hard work, he soon discovered, but fun as well. As they were showing him yet another thing he could help with, he turned to find Reese. And all at once, he fell in love with her.

Not like Parker did. No, they were too good of friends for that, but as a sister, mother, and friend. She had never told him to go away, never asked him to leave her alone in all the time they'd been running. Her last money was spent on keeping him fed and safe. When he needed a break, a bed to rest in, a shower to use, she'd gone out of her way to give it to him. And she'd taught him friendship. Something that he'd never known about until he'd met her.

"She's a beauty, isn't she?" He nodded at Rich. "And about the sweetest person I ever had the pleasure of meeting. I love that Lauren with all that I am, and I know that she's good for us all, but there is a sweetness about Reese that I've only ever seen once, and that is in my own Bea."

"She's happy. I mean, really happy." They watched her as she tried to move the stove that had been brought into the house. When one of the workers picked her up and moved her out of the way, her laughter rang through the room. Several of the others turned to look, smiles on their own faces. "Reese will make this a home for Parker. A good home."

"You sound like you might be leaving here." Josh just looked at the older man. "I don't know if you know this or not, but you leaving here would break her heart. And mine

67

too. Why, just last night me and Bea were talking about what a fine addition you make to our growing family. And when those twins come along, you'll be a cousin to them too."

"I'm not any relation to any of you." Rich told him he was wrong; he was their grandson as far as they were concerned. "You don't know me that well, Rich. For all you know I could be a monster."

"Are you?" Josh waited a heartbeat before he nodded. "You gonna hurt any of us? I'm assuming that you got yourself some control over what you think of as a monster. By the way, you ain't no such thing as a monster. Them men that are chasing you are."

"Sometimes. I've…she doesn't know what I can do." Rich nodded and looked at Reese when he did. "She could be hurt more because of me. You all might be better off without me around."

"I don't think so. And as far as what you can do, I'm sure as I'm standing here that if you do let that thing, whatever it might be, go, you'd never intentionally hurt one of us. And that, as far as I can see, is all we need to know." Josh tried to tell him that he wasn't sure of all he could do. "We'll work on that too. Now you go on and see about getting those shelves hung up. I got to help with the wall that we're putting in the dining room. Gotta expand it for the family."

Josh worked with the men until Parker came in. The kitchen, for the most part, was finished. There wasn't much in the way of food in the cabinets, and the pantry was devoid of anything but the freezer, refrigerator, and shelves, but it was taking shape, looking like someone lived there. And Reese was making dinner for everyone.

~~~

At midnight, Parker was sitting in his living room on a

lawn chair. The furniture for this room had been put in the barn when the walls had been taken down. He had only said in passing that he wanted a fireplace in the big room, and within minutes someone was shouting out orders to get the things out of the way. He smiled when Reese came in the room with a glass of tea for them both.

"The dining area is all taped off now. Your dad and brother said they'd be back in the morning." He said he'd spoken to them both. "I never meant for this to be blown up like this. I only called your dad to see if he could tell me how to hang up a few of the cabinets."

"It's great. I should have let him come help me sooner. I guess I thought I had to do it on my own. But I know now that I couldn't have. Not in a million years." She sat on the room's only other piece of furniture, another lawn chair. "Are you okay with the fireplace in this room?"

"Yes. I mean, I never even considered it, but I can see it now." They both looked at the wall where the shaft for the thing had been put in. "The men that were here today, they sure do know their business."

"They do. Dad and Dustin have gotten really good at redoing houses. They also remodel homes for other people. Dustin was doing all right before he asked Dad if he wanted to invest so he could buy a truck, and it took off after that. I'm really glad they could come and help us."

"Me too. I learned so much today." He nodded. "Your mom, she said that she'd help us out for tomorrow when it came to feeding them all. Did you know that Lauren is working at sorting out the lab?"

The change in subject threw him off a little, but he told her that he did. "She's been talking with her boss, and he wants it shut down, but also wants her to take care that it can't be opened again."

"Her boss. You make it sound like she works for Joe Businessman. I didn't believe her at first when she said she works for the president. Of the United States. But when he called here, asking for Josh, I was shocked." Parker laughed and asked her to come and sit with him. "I don't know if you realize it or not, but that chair is not made for two people."

"It can be if you sit on my lap and ride me." He'd meant it as a joke. But the moment that her eyes brightened up, he sat up and told her to come to him. "Take off all your clothing too. I want to eat you while you stand here."

"Parker. You make me insane." But she did as he asked, standing up and moving toward him as she unbuttoned her blouse. "When I woke up this morning in your bed, all I could think about was all the things you'd done to me last night. And this morning."

"I loved waking you up with a climax. Christ, all I could think about when you came was how much I loved you." She stopped moving and he sat up on the chair. "I do love you, Reese. I know you might find that hard to believe, but it's true."

"You mentioned your cat to me. How he wanted to have his time with me." He nodded, not sure where she was going but hoping he knew. He didn't even mind the change in subject again. "I'd like that, I think. To see how many times he can make me come."

He let his cat consume him. It wasn't hard for him to do that, but he'd forgotten he was sitting in a lawn chair. The plastic of the seat tangled up in his paws, and then he fell over with it on his back.

"Here, let me help you." His cat sat still when Reese came toward them. He warned him to go carefully with her, she wasn't used to him yet. "Next time you shift, you should take better care of your surroundings."

When she'd gotten them untangled, his cat rubbed his head over her neck and shoulder. He wasn't sure what he was doing—marking her for sure—but he was being so gentle with her, like he was a big kitten in her lap. And when she hugged him to her, just wrapped her arms around him and held the big cat, Parker could feel her happiness.

*She is wonderful. And has accepted me as her mate as well. You couldn't do any better than her, I think.* Parker told his cat that he loved her as well. *Good. When we convert her, she'll be safer.*

Standing up, his cat swiped at her pants. When they were in shreds around her waist, Parker spoke to her through their link. If she was startled by it, she didn't say.

*He wants you to be naked. So do I, as a matter of fact.* She pulled her blouse up and over her head, and then tore her pants off the rest of the way. *If we keep this up, you're going to be naked all the time. Perhaps we should think of buying you some more clothing soon.*

"I don't want to talk about clothing right now." She took off her bra, then her panties, and was standing there naked, beautifully so. "I'm afraid. I have no idea what to expect from this, but I'm excited and afraid at the same time."

*Spread your legs for us. If you need to lie down, you can do that too.* She sat down on the floor, her body trembling a little. *If we had the fireplace in, I'd turn it on to warm you up.*

"I have a feeling that I'm going to be pretty warm here in a bit." He hoped so too as his cat made his way to her. "Parker, he won't hurt me, will he?"

*Never.*

His cat seemed to understand she was frightened of him. So he laid down, his big head on her abdomen, and she ran her fingers though his fur. As soon as she seemed to settle down, he moved to be between her outstretched legs.

He could smell her. Not just her fear, that was a given, but her need as well. Then when his cat licked her from gate to clit, she cried out twice. Her body was tense with her unleashed passion now, bowing up from the floor with each of his strokes. And when she came, screaming out his name, the big cat purred and brought her a second, then a third time.

Reese came for them several more times before his cat let him go. As Parker buried his own mouth over her, she held him to her, begging him to stop and asking for more at the same time. When she told him she was done, that she wasn't able to come again, he moved up her body, nipping and kissing every part of her he could reach.

Parker tasted the curve of her body, her nipple, and breast. He nipped at her ribs, licking a path from her side to her sternum. Her skin was dewy, salty, and warm. He loved every part of her; the way her breath caught when he bit too hard; how she chewed on her lower lip when she was close to coming. There was nothing about this woman, his woman, that he didn't love.

"You're so beautiful." She shook her head, pulling his mouth to hers. When he devoured as much of her as he could, he lifted his head and slid deep inside of her. "Mine. You're all mine."

"And you are mine." He made love to her slowly, keeping her close to the edge but not letting her fall over. Not yet. He was ready too, and had to slow his own heart beat a couple of times when it felt as if it were leaving his chest.

He loved her; all of her, every pore, every cell of her. And when she came, calling out his name as she held him, Parker fell more deeply in love with her as he filled her again and again.

Later, when he could move without hurting himself, he rolled over then stood up. His clothing was torn to shreds, as was hers, but he picked her up in his arms and carried her to their room. It was just a mattress on the floor at this point, but he was going to remedy that in the morning.

As soon as her head touched the pillow, she looked up at him and smiled. "Will you marry me?" He nodded, then smiled at her when she rolled over and curled up. "Good. I'd like children too someday."

Parker sat there for over an hour just watching her sleep. He had opened up his computer some time ago, and now it had gone to sleep waiting for him to make a move. Clicking on a few of the websites that he'd been looking at before Reese had come into his life, he made different choices, made purchases with the two of them in mind rather than himself.

By the time the sun was coming up, he was ready for his day. It was going to be a long one, what with no sleep, but he was excited for it. Getting out of the shower, he was disappointed to find the mattress empty, but dressed anyway, knowing that wherever she went, she'd be safe. Going to the kitchen, following his nose all the way, he was grateful to see not just her in the kitchen making breakfast, but Josh as well. The boy wanted to help him out today in the fields.

"I've never been around wild animals before." Parker told him they weren't so much wild as they were tamed. "Either way, I'd like to go and help you as much as I can. Perhaps you can show me how to milk a cow."

"We have cattle on the hoof; they're sold for the meat, not for milking." The disappointment on his face had Parker wishing he had one cow just for the kid to milk. "But I know that a friend of mine has several milkers. He wants to use one of the studs for his farm, so maybe we can work something out with him. I don't know how to milk one either. I think he might use a system, but we'll see."

Excitement was running high in the house before he left. Josh was dressed for the chill of the morning, and was ready to strip down in the afternoon when it got hotter. Reese made them both thick sandwiches to take with them, and several bottles of water. He wanted to tell her that he normally just ate some jerky or whatever was left over from the night before, but kissed her on the cheek and left with a bounce in his step. He could get used to this really quickly.

As they made their way to the barn, he saw the dust flying up on the drive. Telling Josh to go back to the house, he reached out to his brothers when the boy flew away. No one would be coming up his drive this early in the morning without a good reason. As soon as he was sure that Josh was safe, he moved to hide the rig by closing up the barn doors, and waited by the fence around his paddock. Bear and a couple more of the shifters on his land came out to join him. Bear told him he was armed, as were the rest of them if he needed them.

"I don't know anything right now. But thanks." Almost as soon as he saw the car and that there were no plates on the front of it, he knew he was in deep shit. "Get Lauren here, as well as the rest of them, please. And at all costs, protect my family."

"Done. And Lauren is on her way." He nodded as the three men got out of the big black car. "Also, you might want to know that they ain't going nowhere until we let them. The drive is blocked."

Parker had no idea why that was important but didn't ask. The back door to the car was opened and he watched as a man rolled out. Christ, he was fucking huge. And as he made his way to him, looking all around as he did so, Parker told Reese to stay in the house.

*No problem there. Your mom and dad are here. I don't think they're none too happy with these guys either. Your mom, she is really scary when she's pissed, isn't she?* He asked her if they were cat or human. *Human. But your dad said he can change faster than a clicker on the television if need be. He does know that clickers aren't around anymore, doesn't he?*

*He does. There are times when I swear he's been in a time warp. Just be safe for me.* She told him she would if he would. *I will. But this guy has to know he's in over his head here.*

# Chapter 6

Charles Dodson wasn't sure what he had expected when he'd been told about this place. The house was beautiful, large, and charming. There were no couches on the front porch, nor did he see a hundred dogs in the yard. All things he'd seen on television when he'd had to watch something with his family. As he made his way to the fence where several men stood, he tried to judge who was in charge and who was going to do as he wanted. Right now it was a tossup between the taller man in the middle and the one standing next to the barn doors.

"Hello. I'm here on a mission I hope you can help me with." No one said a word to him, nor did they take his offered hand. "I assure you, I'm not here to sell you anything."

"Yes you are. Bullshit, I'm thinking. It's not even seven in the morning and here you are on my land uninvited. Sounds to me like anything you might have to say is going to be bullshit." Charles wanted to slap the man, but only smiled tightly at him. "What is it you want, Mr. Dodson?"

Charles started to explain why he was there when he realized that they knew his name. Not sure how to proceed

77

now that he'd been found out, he wondered if the man knew what he was there for. Instead of the little song and dance he had in mind with this man, if he was indeed the owner, Charles got right to business.

"I think you might know a friend of mine. Savage is what he goes by now. And a woman, her name is Reese Farley. I'd like to talk to them." The man didn't move but the bigger man did, shifting on his feet in a way that made Charles nervous. "Perhaps we can go indoors and talk this over. What I have to say to you is private, and I think we'd be more comfortable sitting down, don't you?"

"No. No I don't. And we're just fine and dandy right where we are. However, if you could see your way into getting back in your car and leaving, that would be better." Charles didn't like being told no. And he hated being put into a position where he had to hold his temper. But he wanted something from this man and he was by God going to give it to him. "Listen Charlie, you should go now or I'm going to have to call the police."

"It's not Charlie, but Charles. And if you'd done your homework as I have, then you'd know that, Parker McCullough." He had to bite the inside of his cheek to keep from pulling out his gun and using it on him. "I don't know how you found out my name, and I'd hoped we'd be civilized about this, but I can see that you aren't going to be. So I would like it if you kept it formal. You may call me Mr. Dodson."

"And you can call me Kiss My Ass. Or Mr. Fuck You. I don't care. So long as we're formal, you know. But, I want you out of here. I don't know why you've come all the way out here in the first place, but you're trespassing and I want you gone." The man stood up and Charles realized that him leaning against the fence had hidden a great deal about the man. "You're not welcome here."

McCullough was taller than Dodson's own six foot five inches by another four or five inches. He was broader too. Not fat, like the few pounds that Charles had put on in recent years, but muscled. And not the kind you'd get from a gym, but from hard work. Charles tried a different approach, one that he'd been told to use in the first place. Good old boy act.

"You're not terribly sociable are you, Mr. McCullough? And here I thought you and your five brothers were about as nice as they came." He wanted to prove to the man that he had resources as well. Ones that could dig deep into a life and find out the worse kind of secrets. Not that this family had any that he could find, but he was still looking. "That sister-in-law of yours, she tell you who I am? Not very sporting of her, now is it. I just want what is mine, and hope that we can come to some kind of mutual financial understanding."

There was a noise behind him and he turned in time to see two of his men drop to the ground. His driver, Phillip, dropped a few seconds later. Charles started to run to the men in front of him, to hide behind them if necessary, but he was stopped by something touching the back of his head. The gun, unmistakable now that someone had pushed it deeper into his flesh, wouldn't miss.

McCullough laughed before speaking. "Well, Charlie, I'd like you to meet my sister-in-law. Lauren, this is the man we were just talking about." He started to turn, to demand that she back off, but she told him to stop where he was. "She has been going over some of the paperwork at the lab, and you'd be surprised how many times your name has come up."

"What are you talking about? You were trespassing? You're responsible for the mess I just left there? Damn it, do you have any idea how much trouble you've caused me by

79

going into my labs?" Lauren laughed and so did the big man. "What the fuck do you think you're doing? I came out here to talk to you."

"I've closed it down, by order of the president." He turned when the woman spoke, despite the bite of the gun to his head. "That's right. We've gone in and closed you up. Taken all the computers, specimens, as well as any notes that might have been there. I do believe that as of early this morning, an order was put out that you were to be arrested on sight. I've decided to have a little fun with you until I get some answers."

"Where is Fritz? Has he been arrested too?" Lauren told him he was missing. "Missing? How the fuck did you let that happen? Missing how? Did you shoot him and then bury his body in the back yard so that no one would find him?"

"Good idea, but no, he's just missing. We have a line on where he might be, but for now he's not in jail." She grinned at him. "But you'll do nicely in the meantime."

"I'm not going to jail." She only grinned at him and he looked at the man again. "What is wrong with you people? Don't you see that this is bigger than any of you? That what we're doing there will save lives? Make our military one of the greatest? You people and your backwater way of thinking is what got us to be the laughingstock of the entire world. You of all people should know that we're just not that good anymore."

"Funny, but I thought that we already were the greatest." He huffed at her, not at all understanding how she could be so dense. "You really think that creating a human being that would withstand a direct hit to the head is the way to go? That messing with the natural order of things is something to be proud of? Not that you're going to get the chance to try again, but I'm wondering if you have any idea of the danger that could arrive from fucking with someone you don't fully understand."

"You of all people should have figured out what we're doing there. We need an army that people will fear. A group of men that, no matter what, will come out on top." He thought of her own record. "You would never have been hurt when you were over there. The things that I'm creating would never have turned on each other. You would have been one of the few I would have changed given the chance. Give me back my notes and my lab and I'll make you the greatest solider that ever lived."

He was picked up. As he hung from the air, all he could think about was that he was going to die. Then he realized that neither of the people he'd been talking to was touching him. No one was. When he was turned, his body just moving without any sort of effort from himself, he looked at the boy he'd been checking on weekly for years. SA-8.

He was surrounded in a bright light, his hair standing on end, arms lifted in the air. When he realized that it was him holding him, his power keeping him from moving, Charles was proud in that moment. He'd been a part of something so great that no one would ever believe it.

"Josh, let him go." Parker, if he remembered the name right, was standing between him and his greatest creation. Not even the birth of his children had meant as much as this did to him. "Josh, he's not worth it. Let him go."

"Do you have any idea what he did to me? What he ordered done to me and the others?" Parker said that he didn't but he'd be willing to talk about it. "He made me, made me what I am. Then he tried to destroy me when they thought me a failure."

"Is that why you ran?" The grip of power around his

throat tightened when he tried to explain to the creation that it would never happen now. But Parker seemed to understand something that he shouldn't have been privy to. "You got out when they thought to kill you. Because you knew that if they tried you would have destroyed them. And Reese too. Because she was there."

"I could feel her, her kindness, her struggles to be nice to the man screaming at her. It wasn't her fault that the lab had been shorted something." Parker said he understood that too. Charles tried to speak again. He wanted them to know that nothing would happen to SA-8 ever again. But they'd forgotten him for some reason. "She was nice."

Charles was feeling lightheaded; his body was weakening with the grip around his throat. And almost as soon as he thought he was going to die this way, he was released, his body dropping to the ground. But he got no further than standing up, holding onto his car, when he was manhandled again. As he was being shoved against his car, his head nearly smashed into the metal, his men were also being detained. Charles started to tell them again that SA-8 was his. No one was listening to him.

These people were going to pay for their treatment of him. He was going to be praised for his work. Countries were going to pay him top dollar for coming and showing them how to make this thing he'd had a part in. The president was going to apologize to him and the world for what they'd done to his lab. Charles Dodson was going to be known throughout history as the man who had created the greatest army in the world.

"Charles Dodson, you're under arrest." As the list of things was named off, he watched the young man calm, saw how Parker interacted with him to bring his power down. He could use a good man like him and would see about recruiting him. Maybe he'd even see about getting that butch of a woman to come and head up his security. The president would give him the world once he found out what he'd done.

While being shoved in the back of the cruiser, all he could think about was that Fritz's disappearance could not have come at a better time. He was glad now that he'd not bothered calling Doc about any of this either. He was sure that he'd find out soon enough, but by the time he got up off his fat ass and made it here, Charles would have convinced them all he was the scientist and creator. Instead of sharing the limelight with either man, he was now going to have it all. Yes, sir, he thought, Charles Dodson was going to be a very famous man soon.

~~~

Parker wasn't sure who to talk to about what had just happened. Josh had been ready to kill that man. And he had stupidly stepped in front of him. Parker reached for the glass on the table again and saw that his hand, while still trembling, wasn't as bad as it had been.

"Josh is laying down." Parker nodded and sat the glass down after drinking from it. "I've never seen him do that before. What made you think to talk to him? I think I might have run for the hills."

"He was going to kill that man." Reese said she thought so as well. "I couldn't let him do that. Not kill anyone, but especially not that man."

"Why not that man? And I'm not saying that you're wrong, but why not that man? From what Josh has told me, they weren't very nice to him there. And he said that man in particular, while not there often, treated him like a thing, not a person." Josh had told him that his name in the lab had been

SA-8. It was how he'd come up with Savage as a last name. "Parker, that man, he's talking like he's going to be free soon."

"He won't be. Lauren said he's been put in maximum security and won't be seeing the light of day for a long time." She nodded, not looking convinced. "Have you talked to Josh about things that went on there? I mean, has he talked to you about what they did to him?"

"I don't think he was taken there. He's never said, but I think perhaps they made him there." Parker nodded. He'd gotten that from Lauren. She knew all the details of his creation. "He's not even a shifter, is he? I mean, I saw what he could do today and he can shift, but that's not all he can do, is it?"

"No, it's not. According to Lauren he can manipulate computers, people, as well as animals. They didn't know this, of course, until the end of his time there, but there were extensive tests done on him. Apparently Josh kept a great deal from them as well." She asked him if it was what had happened today to one of them. "Yes. There is no mention of him having the kind of power he displayed today. They knew that he could lift objects, pretty heavy ones. That he could read minds when they were close enough. The lab was set to destroy him the day he got away. And leaving was the only way he knew to save you and himself. He thought that if they tried to kill him, which I'm thinking isn't possible, that you would have been killed as well. He liked you very much."

"Why me?" He told her what Josh had told him out in the yard. "So because I was nice to the people I unloaded food for, he came to me? I don't believe that. I'm nothing special."

"You were to him. I mean, even though he'd never met you, he knew what I know about you now. Your kindness. How you are around people. Even the fact that you were willing to lay your life on the line for him, he could see that in you." Parker pulled her from her chair and put her on his lap. The need to be touched by her, to touch her, was overwhelming. "Josh is exactly what they wanted when they made him."

"He thinks he's a monster." Parker said that his dad told him that as well. "He's not a monster. He's a kid that has been dealt a shitty hand and not given any way to fix it."

"That's about right. Do you want to know what they found out at the lab?" She said that she wasn't sure. "I wasn't either, but Lauren said it might help us when he has questions. I'm pretty sure that he has some about now."

"I'm sure." When she got up from his lap and started pulling things from the cabinets, he watched her. "I don't want to know right now, if it's okay with you. Later. When things are more settled."

Parker got up and wrapped his arms around her. Holding her like this, her head under his chin, he actually felt like he would be able to handle this. Whatever this might be. When someone knocked at the door, he turned so that she was behind him, protecting her with his body when he saw his dad. He did not look happy.

"I've been a thinking about those men today. And I have to tell you, son, your momma and I are really upset." Parker nodded. "Damned men are gonna make me have to get all pissy with them."

His dad never cursed. Never. He told him that to curse like a man on leave made you look stupid, like you had not the sense to get in out of the rain. And now, some bastard had made him not curse once, but twice in the same minute. Parker hugged his dad tightly when he told him he wanted to talk to his grandson.

After his dad made his way to Josh's room, Parker went

back out to the barn. He really was behind now and had a lot of work to catch up on. As he pulled his tractor out of the barn after gassing it up and making sure it was fit to run, he was surprised and pleased to see Josh coming out of the house.

"Grandda said that I should come on out and help you. That if I was given the opportunity to hit something, that I should do it." Parker moved over and showed Josh where to stand on the back end of the tractor. "Thank you for what you did today for me. I don't know why you did it, but I'm thankful that you did."

"Because you're my family." Josh nodded and Parker shook his head. "No, I'm not just saying that, Josh. I have begun to think of you as my son. I know that it's not been a long time since we met, but you mean the world to me. To all of my family."

The hay had been brought out to the field yesterday and was waiting to be stowed away. He showed Josh how to spread the older stuff around, moving the cattle around to that they didn't block others from having some of it too. Then they filled the water trough for those that were heavy with babies. Right now he had six that were ready to drop, and two more that he was hoping would be pregnant in a few weeks. His cattle were a good source of income for his ranch, and he took care of them like he might family. And the stud service money that he got went right into the bank for the ranch.

Not that he needed to work the ranch so that it was viable. They were all rich, wealthy as Midas, as his mom would say. But they also knew that in a heartbeat they could lose it all, for one reason or another. And he enjoyed the work. There were days that he'd gladly trade for one of his brothers' jobs, but for the most part, it was what he enjoyed doing so he gave it all he had. It was the way all his brothers did when they worked. To do less would be disappointing.

"Do you suppose one day they'll stop looking for me?" Josh looked at him pleadingly, and as much as he wanted to assure him that they would, he told him he had no idea. "It's been my fantasy to have my own home. A place that I could live without fear of someone coming to take me away."

"No one is going to take you so long as I can keep you safe." Josh nodded. "My entire family is here for you, Josh. We're not going to let anyone hurt you if we can help it. And a home is a very admirable thing to want. It's something no one can take away from you so long as you take care of it, make the payments."

"I can protect myself, you know." Parker knew that first hand. "But I'm lonely without you guys. I thought...."

"You thought what?" Parker waited for him to finish, but when it didn't appear that he was going to answer him, he changed the subject, to give him time. "My dad said you did a great job on mudding the drywall. He said that once you get this all cleared up he'd very much like to have you come and work for him. He has it in his head that he's getting too old for such a job."

"Too old. The man can outwork most of the crew that works for him and Dustin. He's amazing. Yesterday, when the cabinets were hung, he realized that he'd put them in the wrong order. I didn't know what he meant; I'd never even been near a cabinet that didn't have chemicals or other stuff like that in them. But he had me help him take them down and put them back up before anyone noticed. And as soon as we had them up, I could see it then. They *were* in the wrong order. The doors were what gave it away. They didn't open to each other." Josh spread out another bale of hay before turning to him again. "Last night I thought I could just leave here. You'd never be able to find me, not if I didn't want you to. But I couldn't do it. I had to come back and see this through. For you guys."

"I'm glad you did." Parker told him how much they'd all miss him, and regardless of whether or not they'd be able to find him, they'd still try. "You can't just walk out on family without us worrying about you. Don't leave us, Josh. I think it would break my dad's heart if you did."

"Yeah, mine too." As they finished up the job at hand, Parker told him what else they had to do today. Like checking on the field nearest the river. "I can do that."

"I don't know. It's pretty far away." Josh said he could do it from the sky. Just needed to know what he was looking for. "When we have a lot of rain, the river can come up pretty fast and sometimes the cattle get stuck out on this little area of land that gets surrounded. Once the water starts to go back down, the stupid animals don't have the sense to come back across it. I've had to go out there several times and bring the lead over the water to safer grounds."

In the end, Parker and Josh went to the river. He not thought of him not knowing how to swim, and Parker was afraid of the current if Josh had to go out and guide the animals across. The water could be rough at times and could take him under. Josh was so excited to be learning to swim when they got out there, Parker didn't tell him that the water would be too cold this time of year.

The cattle were rescued from themselves, and the two of them had a good time in the shallow water. On their way back to the barn Josh told him he would never leave them, and that he'd protect them too. Parker thought it was a good day. A short one, but a good one altogether.

Before they were even in the house he could see the

difference. Empty boxes were all over the place, and the dumpster that had been brought out was heavy with more cardboard and Styrofoam than he'd thought he had. He'd have to call someone in the morning to come and empty it for them. Parker looked around the outside of his home and felt his pride swell up.

The wall had been replaced in the dining room, he could see now, and the big french doors were open to the evening air. He could smell dinner cooking and the men at the hose cleaning up for a bite of whatever he was smelling. Parker looked over at Josh when he laughed.

"She said that when we got back we'd have a feast. I'm thinking that regardless of the fact that she's feeding twenty others, she's having the time of her life." Parker thought so as well. "And just so you know, she wants to open her own place someday. A little diner like the one in town."

"Did you know that it's for sale?" Josh said that he did know that. "Well then, I think we can help her out by seeing to that, don't you?"

"She's gonna have a brick, you know that, don't you? I mean, she's been talking about it since I first got to know her." Parker said he was going to talk to Margaret and May in the morning. "Good for you and for us. We might have to go there for a few meals, but she'll be happy with it. And a happy Reese is a relaxed Reese."

Parker cleaned up in the kitchen with Josh. His mom and dad were there too, and his dad looked to be in a much better mood. Mom told him he'd been so upset that that man had tried to hurt Josh that he'd wanted to go downtown to the jail and tear him apart. Another first for his dad. He wasn't a violent man.

"Is this all right?" He asked Reese what she meant when

she cornered him in the kitchen. "Feeding all these people. I mean, just look how much work they've gotten done in two days. I thought the least we could do was feed them."

"I think it's just wonderful. And you can feed them every night if you want." She grinned at him. "All right, not every night, but on the weekends if they come over to work. They do eat a lot."

She was still laughing when he took the largest bowl of mashed potatoes he'd ever seen from her. Makeshift tables had been set up in the yard to accommodate them all, and Colin and the rest of them had shown up with chairs to use. It was going to be so wonderful having his family over all the time. Parker couldn't wait until Thanksgiving.

# CHAPTER 7

Fritz was going crazy. He was bored out of his mind, and starving to death eating only canned things. And he'd discovered that he was a failure at gardening. Christ, could this be any worse? he wondered, not for the first time since he'd entered this place.

The very first day he'd forgotten that he had to turn on the water pump and the air circulation system. He'd taken a big dump in the toilet only to have the smell of it remain in the place for hours. And no matter how many times he'd pushed the fucking button to flush, it wouldn't work. It had taken him nearly six hours of living in the stench before he found the instructions on how to use it.

"Mother fuckers should have put that kind of information right over the commode." He wandered through the five rooms, all five of them no bigger than his own closet had been. "And I should have known that I'd have no time to pack before coming down here."

He'd had a few things in the cell, as he'd been calling it. Some clothing that he'd brought down and left when he'd been experimenting with staying here overnight. He had food of course, but not much of it was fit to eat. Canned pasta. Microwave dinners. It was nasty shit but all he had. And he couldn't just throw it out; it was marked as portions, and if he ate too much or threw out what he didn't like to start over, then he was going to starve. Staying down here for any length of time was going to be scary if he didn't have any food to eat. As it was, he was bored to death with his own company.

The television didn't work half the time. He was reasonably sure there were instructions to that as well, but he hadn't bothered looking. Fritz hadn't been one for sitting around watching mindless shit on it anyway, and being bored wasn't going to change that. But he did have his computer. And so long as he was careful to plug it in every night, he had enough power to run it nearly all day. On the upper level, he'd had people do that for him.

Going to his computer now, he looked around his office as it came online. It was so small in here, tight as a rug, as his grandma had said, and he hated it too. If ever he had to be in one of these things again, he was going to take better care of the amount of room he had and the furniture that was in it. Christ, this cheap shit was for the birds.

As soon as his computer came online he saw that he had over one hundred emails. Smiling to himself, he had wondered if they would miss his input on things. People would wonder if he was all right. He was even guessing that about now Charles or Doc was looking for him. The two of them couldn't do anything without his say-so or approval.

The first email he opened was from someone by the name of Winslow. He didn't know who that was so he only scanned the content. Something about court dates and appearing before a committee. Well, that shit wasn't going to happen.

He was going to stay right where he was until this thing blew over.

The next few were from contractors. They wanted money for projects that they'd done for the lab. Well, they were going to be out of luck too if that woman was right. The more he thought about it, the less he thought anything at all had happened really. For all he knew it was a scam to get into the lab and steal from him. Drugs, he'd bet anything. Fritz glanced over at the bag he'd brought down with him.

It had been filled with comic books. Not when he'd loaded it a few months ago, but now it was. Comic books that he'd seen as a kid, stupid ones about kids growing up with dumb names like Archie, and some about a girl rock band as well. A few of them were even about a family of ghosts. But not one file or folder about his work above. Nothing at all.

Whoever had it—and he wasn't sure who at this point—had all his notes on everything. Not just the work done in the lab—that was bad enough—but names as well. Who had donated their sperm, when and how. There were notes on SA-8 that he knew would get him into trouble if they could figure out his code.

Not that it was a hard code to break. He'd written it down on the first page of his notes so that he'd not forget it. Christ, if there was a dumber criminal than him, he wasn't sure he ever wanted to meet them. But he did have this, his hidey hole.

As he continued to look over his mail, he kept seeing the name Winslow. Finally, after skimming over ten or more, he opened the last one. Fritz was nearly half way through it when he realized it had an attachment that he was supposed to open and fill out if he couldn't make the appointed court date.

He had seen scams like this one before. All a person had to do was open the attachment and all sorts of terrible things could happen. Such as they'd take all your money. Or take over your computer so that you'd have to pay to be able to access it. Fritz thought he might be a little off, but he wasn't that stupid. So instead of doing any of that, he decided to set up a filter that would delete emails from Winslow as soon as they hit his inbox. The ding of his notifications startled him.

*You are a moron. I'm sure that someone along the line has pointed that out to you, but it should be pointed out again. You're a moron.*

He wasn't sure who would have left him such a message so he clicked out of it. Messenger wasn't something he was overly fond of anyway, and he wasn't going to get trapped in a verbal war game today. But it came back online immediately.

*Did you know that all the people who worked for you have been arrested? Does that bother you at all? Not that I give two shits if it bothers you at all, but the people here think you should. How dumb are they? Hmmm. You think they know you left them there without a single backup plan for them?*

Engaging with someone online, he knew, was wrong. But he also knew that he was safe here, there was no way anyone was going to be able to get his code. Only he knew it and it was tamper proof. So he decided that he was just bored enough to talk to this person.

"No," he typed. Then he decided to find out who the fuck this was. "I don't know who you think you're talking to, but we have no business at all to discuss. I'd very much appreciate it if you left me alone."

*Oh, but we do, Fritz. We have a great deal of business to discuss, you and I.* That fucking woman again. He nearly closed out of the email when she sent another message. *It was pretty clever of you to have put yourself in a bomb shelter. We didn't see that one coming. Good for you. But now that we have, we're coming for you.*

He looked around, wondering how he would escape if she really did come to get him. There was a flight hole, a way out in the back, but he wasn't really sure where it led. Fritz was fuzzy on a lot of details about this place.

"They should have had a plan. I did and now look, I'm safe." He put a little smiley face at the end of his message before hitting enter.

*Cute. So, you have no problem with the hundreds of people's lives you've fucked up with this lab? Or the lives taken in the name of progress? I'm at a loss to think how you thought this was progress, by the way. I knew you were a fucking idiot, but not this stupid.*

"I'm not an idiot. It's because you aren't as forward thinking as I have been that you'd label me as such. Can you imagine a world where there are no wars? No loss of life because someone gets a burr up their ass about something?" He smiled as he continued. Fritz loved explaining his plan to the uneducated. "With our research there will be a single being, a non-human that can go into any situation because he can blend in and take care of our enemies. Destroy those that think to bomb us, take from our lands, or even kidnap those that are important to our world."

*And you get to decide who is important? Who are our enemies? I don't think that's right, do you? I mean, you can't even be trusted to keep your own employees safe, much less an entire nation of them. As I said, you're a fucking moron.* He started to answer her yes, he was the one who decided, when she continued on her end. *And this non-human, are you talking about the boy who escaped from your labs? He pretty much proved that you have no control over dick, didn't he?*

"There was no escape. He was misled by that woman, and we're going to get our project back as soon as possible. SA-8 was our greatest accomplishment. And as soon as all

95

this dies down, and people like you realize what a wonderful creation it is, then I'll prove to the world what I've done." He looked around his little rooms. "You've put me in a position that I cannot continue with my work. What do you suppose the people who fund me are going to think about that?"

*You mean Dodson? Or a few other names on your list? Fritz, I think they're going to be pretty fucking pissed at you when we arrest them. Because we are, just as soon as we can.* He'd forgotten that she had his notes. *Also, he has a name, this SA-8 person that you've fucked with. Did you know that?*

"We don't name monsters. He is a thing, a weapon. To name him would have given him worth. He has no worth other than what he can do for me. For us." Fritz wondered who had given his creation a name. That trucker, no doubt. While SA-8 had been smart, brilliant even, he'd not had much experience with the way things worked. He watched the little curser at the bottom of his messenger as it said the person was typing. Fritz was excited to see what she was going to postulate on next. No doubt the moral implications of what he'd done.

He sat there for nearly half an hour. Nothing else came from her. There was no more name calling and she didn't tell him what a fool he was. All things he had clever answers written down for. But the curser just blinked. Deciding to piss her off more, he starting typing, smiling the entire time at his statements to her.

"Have I rendered all your thoughts as invalid? Have you given up so easily?" Nothing. He wanted her to talk to him, engage in a way that would take some of the boredom away. The longer he sat there, waiting and staring at the little blinking line, the more upset he became. How dare her ignore him like this.

"Come on now. You must have some comment. You have to have an opinion. Even if it's an uneducated one, I'm betting that you have something to say." He waited and waited, and finally let his temper rule his fingers. "Listen, you fucking cunt, you know you're wrong about this. Just fucking return my things and I'll get back to work. I'm not going to ask you a second time."

*Seven, four, three, Alpha, Tango, Zulu.*

He stared at the words there, his heart in his throat when he realized what he was seeing. 743ATZ was his code to get into his domain.

~~~

Reese pulled the pie from the oven and set it on the countertop that had been set in this morning. She looked around the kitchen at all the new appliances, as well as the table and chairs that had been put together and set up. Every square inch of the new kitchen was covered in baked goods. And the few feet that wasn't had the makings for future baked goods ready to be popped in the oven. When someone cleared their throat, she looked up at Parker.

"I can assume that when you're upset or stressed, you bake." She nodded. "And this baking, do you have a plan for it? I mean, I love that you baked — twelve pies and three cakes — but I'm pretty sure that we can't eat all that before it goes bad."

"I couldn't stop." He just leaned against the doorjamb. "When Lauren told me that she knew where Henderson was, all I could think about was he was going to get out and come after Josh and I again. Then I thought about your family and how they would be affected by this. And I guess the new babies too. What will happen to them?"

"Okay. Henderson isn't going anywhere soon. While she

knows how to get to him, she thinks, and I agree, that he is better off down there stewing. Because after a while, he'll begin to think he needs to get out. He's not a man who will go quietly in the night." Reese nodded and pulled the next batch of cookies from the oven when the timer went off. Parker took three of them off the cooling rack as she put them on it, and set them on a plate. "If he comes here, which I don't think he'll even try, he'll be met with all sorts of kick ass people that will, if you keep this up, be too fat to do much more than just shoot him. I would if I had a gun. Are these peanut butter?"

"Yes. I was going to drizzle melted chocolate on them, but you couldn't wait." He nodded as he poured himself a glass of milk. When Josh joined them in the kitchen, he did the same thing, sitting down to half a dozen of the still warm cookies before she could finish them. "You two should know better than to have dessert before dinner."

"I don't think there is room in here for dinner to be made." They all laughed at Josh when he made the observation. "Can we take some of these over to your parents' house? And Grandma Bea asked if you made any more of those coconut cookies, she'd like a batch of them too."

After Parker left to go to the fields, Josh said he was going to his room. Parker had gotten him a bunch of movies from the library and he was catching up on a lot of things that he'd missed. He'd also taken a passion to watching old black and white movies, all of them older than Reese and nearly as old as the elder McCulloughs.

She was putting the last of the pies in the oven, a cherry one this time, when the phone rang. She hadn't even noticed that there was one in the kitchen, but answered it without thinking. The silence on the other end nearly had her hanging up, but then she heard someone talking, telling the caller to speak right fucking now. Then she heard her, her new friend.

"May?" The sob was what got her. "May, are you all right? Is something happening to you?"

"They want you to come down here. Don't do it, darling. I'm not going to be around much longer—"

She was cut off, and the sound of someone hitting a hard object had Reese gripping the handle of the oven door hard, and the phone handle was painful in her other hand. Then another voice came on.

"You'll come to the diner in half an hour. Alone. If I see one person other than you, I'll kill this old broad like I did the first one."

Reese looked up when Josh came in the room with her. When he took the phone from her, she knew that whoever was on the other end thought it was still her. But when Josh spoke, Reese felt the hairs on her arms and neck dance at not just his words, but the delivery of them.

"You will regret this with every breath you take. Which won't be many after I come to you." She heard the man on the phone talking to him, but not what was being said. Then Josh spoke again. "You think I'm a monster now, just wait until I get there."

He laid the phone gently in the cradle and then just stood there. She knew that he was angry; it showed on every part of his body. But when he turned and looked at her, she took a step back. She could see them.

He'd told her once that he'd been mistreated and that he didn't like it when others were too. He'd told her that he could do things, bad things, and since he'd never mentioned it again, she never asked. But now she could see them, every animal, every species that had ever been, right there on his face. When he took a step toward her, his body vibrating with something more, she put up her hand to stop him.

"Don't be afraid of me." She nodded. "I won't hurt you. Not ever. I promise you that. You're as safe with me as you've ever been."

"They want you because of this, what you are." He nodded. "They made you, they did this to you because they could. Because they thought that it was right."

"They wanted a monster. Created me so that I'd be one. I'm not human, you knew that. But I'm so much more." She told him he wasn't a monster. "You thought so a moment ago."

"No. I was frightened, yes, but not because I thought of you as a monster. You're my friend no matter what they did to you." He said nothing. "Josh, what do you plan to do to those people on the phone? You can't kill them."

"Why not? They would have killed you. Gladly. They also killed that very nice elderly woman who did nothing more to them than give us a place to say. And they've threatened you and my family." She started to tell him that it was all right, but he continued before she could. "Don't leave this house. Don't go out there or go to the diner. If you do, you will get hurt."

"You'd hurt me?" He said he'd not mean to. "But don't you see? By going there, hurting or even killing these people, it's going to hurt me too. I don't want you to do this."

"They've given me no choice." She reached for him, wrapping her arms around him as he stood there. And when he finally did the same to her, holding her in his arms, she cried. It was so unfair what they'd done to them all. "Promise me you won't leave here, Reese. Please? I don't want anything to happen to you."

"I won't leave." She reached for Parker and told him what was going on. "Josh, please, I beg of you, don't do this."

He left her there without another word. Just kissed her on the forehead and left. When he was gone, she spoke to Parker again, telling him what she saw and felt right now.

*Josh is going to get hurt.* Parker told her he was on his way into town. *He made me promise that I'd not go there. That I'd stay here so I'd not get hurt.*

*I didn't promise anything. And I'm going to go and help him. However he needs me to.* She cried harder then, sitting in the chair that had been vacant up until a few minutes ago. *My brothers are going into town too. Lauren is coming to you just in case this was a ploy to get you alone. Don't leave until she gets there. All right?*

*Yes. I'll be here.* Reese told him to be careful. *And make sure that the rest of them are aware that Josh might hurt them if they get too close. He won't mean to, but he might.*

*I'll tell them. Love, we're going to make sure that he's all right. I don't know who these people are, but they've fucked with the wrong person if they think they're going to hurt one of mine.*

Reese wanted to go there too, to be there for them both. *You have to come back to me, both of you.*

*We'll do the best that we can. Just stay safe for me.* She promised him that she would. But her heart hurt for them all. Josh was going to be hurt or captured, she just knew it.

She looked around the kitchen at the mess she'd made, and got up to make it right. It was busy work, she knew, but she had to do something. As she was loading the last of the big bowls into the dishwasher, both Lauren and Bea showed up. Reese lost control of her emotions and sobbed out the entire story to them both. When she was finished, Lauren handed her a few sheets of paper.

"I want you to read this. From the beginning to the end. This is the story of the thing they created. It does not refer to

101

him as a person, not once. He was a thing, without feelings or emotion. SA-8 is what he was to them; Josh Savage is who he became despite their efforts." She took the papers and sat down while the two of them sampled the things in the kitchen.

When she'd finished, she looked at Lauren. "Is this true? I mean, this is what you found out that they did to him?"

"Yes. As far as I can tell, this is all true. The day that you took him away, they were set to terminate him. They thought him too soft, too.... Whatever they thought, he was a failure to them. The letters correspond to his name; the S was the next letter in the alphabet to use and the second letter was the same. The way we've calculated it, there have been almost two thousand attempts to come up with what they have in Josh." Reese asked her how she'd come up with that. "They started off with the letter A then another A to start the count. So you'd have AA, then AB and so on. The number after it looks to be the cage number they used. Josh was SA in the eighth cage."

The number of creatures that had been made there was overwhelming. She asked if she knew what had happened to the others, the failures as they called them. Lauren didn't answer and right then, Reese thought she didn't want to know.

"There's more, isn't there? You're holding something back." Lauren nodded but still didn't speak. Reese let her mind wander over all the most horrific things she could think of and looked up at her. "There is more than just Josh."

"Three more that we can figure out. And we haven't been able to find them at the lab. If they are there, whatever means they have to store them are beyond what we've been able to find. There are three doors, all of them under some sort of lock that I can't figure out. We figure that Henderson just might be able to tell us." She asked why they'd not asked him. "Because

102

for now, he's not able to turn them against us, if he can. Right now, I think perhaps we're all safer with them wherever they are until we know for sure that they've not been destroyed."

Three more boys like Josh. Three more creations that might be out there, somewhere, looking for Josh because someone ordered them to. And if they were failures in these men's eyes, what was it about them that deemed them so? As she paced, she thought of something else and turned to the two of them.

"Josh told me once that his mom hadn't died at the hands of the people in the lab. He thought it was protocol that once the woman delivered the babe that they were killed, their use no longer necessary. But his mom disappeared. Why? How?" Lauren pulled out a thick file with the name Josh had been given across it. "Where did you get this?"

"The safe of the bastard in the sublevels." Before she could ask how the fuck she'd gotten those, Lauren handed her another sheet of paper. "She was a witch. Josh's mom wasn't human either, but a witch. And for reasons that I can't explain, I think she's been a bigger part of this than we think."

# CHAPTER 8

Parker could see Josh now. Colin and Dustin were with him, and Larson and Hawkins were on the other side of the street facing the diner. Boyd was hanging back in the event that they needed a doctor. Parker had a feeling that even if Boyd were standing right on top of the victim, when Josh was finished, there would be no helping them.

When a man came out of the diner with May in front of him like a shield, Parker moved to stand next to Josh. "Tell me what the plan is." Josh didn't move, not even to look in his direction. "You have to have a plan, Josh. If not, then this is going to go to shit in a heartbeat."

"They said that they were going to kill May for harboring us. She is as innocent as the rest of you in this. And they already killed Margaret." Parker said that was true. "I don't want anyone to be hurt by this. I'm here to end it."

"This won't end anything and I think you know that." Josh said it would. "No, it won't. There are more men on the list, men who invested in your being made, that are still out there. The government is rounding them up, but there are a lot of them. And it's taking time."

"This will be one less person they have to find." Parker said it would just bring more here. "I don't understand how you can just calmly tell me to walk away."

"I'm not calm at all. If you want to know the truth, Josh, I feel about this close to wetting my pants. And how well do you think that'll go over with the bad guys here?" Josh asked him if he was kidding. "Yes, sort of. But I'm telling you the truth when I say that this won't end well. For any of us. First of all, that man there, he's going to die. But not by your hand. The men in the building, they're going to be shot too. Lauren has men coming in the back now."

"I want to do this." Parker said he could understand that but it wasn't his call. "And if I make it my call? Then what happens? Do I go back to another form of jail? Is that the plan?"

"No, never again. But answer me this; what happens to Reese if you're killed?" Josh looked at him then. "You're not immortal. You can be killed. And then what? All the suffering that Reese went through to make it so you could be free was for nothing. If nothing else, you shouldn't do this for her." Josh looked at the man then back at him. "Josh, killing this man and the others will get you nothing but heartache."

"They won't stop." Parker wasn't going to lie to him and said no, they might not. "So what's to say I just go in there, let them take me or kill me so that this can end? They'd have no one else to go after and would leave you all alone."

"Do you honestly believe that?" Josh didn't say anything but looked at the man in front of him. "Let the others do this. Please?"

Josh only nodded and when he did, the man holding onto May fell back. Blood covered May and her clothing, and two men came out of nowhere to knock her to the ground. The sound of gunfire in the diner was startling, but in seconds it was over. As soon as the men came out, men that worked for his sister-in-law, Parker knew that the good guys had come out on top. At least this time.

They were taken to a remote room. Parker wasn't entirely sure what that meant...he was in the police station in one of the offices. And he was alone. Every time he asked to see Josh he was told momentarily. When the door opened again and he didn't see the kid, Parker did something he'd not done in a very long time; he let his anger rule his cat.

The first man through the door screamed. Parker might have appreciated making a grown man act like a little girl, but he was on a mission. The second officer that tried to stop him was hurt. Not badly, but Parker wondered what sort of idiot would try to stop a nearly three-hundred-pound jaguar with just his hands. As he made his way down the long halls, snarling at whoever got in his way, he thought about Josh and felt the connection.

*I'm at the end of the hall nearest the front of the building. What happened to us letting the others settle this?* Josh was laughing, and for some reason that calmed both Parker and his cat. Turning quickly, he heard the zing of a bullet as it whizzed by his head, and leapt at the man firing at him. *Don't get killed, Parker. Reese will be really mad at you if you do.*

He wasn't sure how to open the door once he got there, but he stood in front of it. No one was going in there without being bloodied. When he saw a man coming at him with a gun out, he snarled at him.

Parker wasn't stupid enough to think he could outrun a bullet. And if the man fired at him, he'd be hit. There wasn't anywhere for him to go. But he saw Lauren and another man

107

coming up behind the guy with the gun, and he heard her tell him to stand down.

"Ma'am, this cat here, he's running lose. A big fucking cat. I've been ordered to shoot to kill." Lauren looked at him as if to say, really? "He's hurt three other officers. How the hell did he get in here? And where did he come from?"

"Do I look like a fucking zoo keeper to you? On my body somewhere, does it say Doolittle, like I'm fucking going to talk to him to find out?" The officer actually looked her over as if making sure. "I told you to stand down, and I don't like having to repeat myself. Bear, see to this idiot before I have to."

As soon as they were alone in the hall, she shook her head at him. Parker didn't care. He had been polite and when no one had helped him, he'd helped himself. He told Lauren the same thing.

"I was coming to see you. And I made sure that Josh was all right. Where is he?" He looked toward the door behind him. "Mother fucking son of a fucking bitch. I told them to put him in.... Someone's head is going to roll for this. Doesn't anyone fucking listen when I speak? Don't they know that I'm way smarter than them?"

He knew she was trying to be funny, that she didn't really believe that she was smarter than anyone. She more than likely was, but she'd never think that. But it had the desired effect. His cat and him were much better now.

She opened the door for him and Josh didn't move. He was curled up in a tight ball in the corner of the room. Parker moved by her, his cat bigger than she was anyway, and laid down next to the boy. When his hand reached out to touch his fur, Parker moved his head to his lap.

"I was sure that I was going back." Parker told him never,

but Lauren spoke then. She told him she had him. "So did that man. Henderson. He would tell me that he had my back, that he'd never let them do more to me than I could stand. I thought…up until the day before I left, I thought he was really looking out for me. But it was him that signed the order for me to be killed. They were going to end me like I wasn't nothing but expired food."

His heart hurt for the younger man. To be treated like nothing, to be thought of as a monster, was too much. When he sat there, not moving, Lauren came in the room with them and sat on the floor across from them. When she spoke in low tones, both of them watched her.

"When I was first in the service after boot camp, what now seems like a million years ago, I was told that we had a search and rescue. Simple, they told us. In and out. And it was, to a point." The fingers in his fur stopped and tightened for just a moment before they were moving again. "What no one counted on, and we'd never been trained on, was that the man didn't know how to leave. He'd been there for so long, about eight years before we went for him, and he had no clue how to be a human being again. Not that he wasn't…human, I mean, but he'd lost his ability to be one. He had been a captive just long enough, he told us, that he'd lost his humanity. You are not like him."

"I feel it." Lauren told him that was good, to feel. "I was in a cage for the biggest part of my life. And when not in a cage about the size of this room, I was in a lab setting. No one spoke to me but to tell me to stand or sit. I ate what was put in front of me, and knew what day of the week it was by what I ate. Ham on Monday. Spaghetti on Tuesday. It was never ending, never changing, and I was used to it."

"Then you found a phone in your room." He nodded and

asked her how she'd known that. "Notes. I have all the notes on your progress, the failures they thought you had and what was done to you. If you'd like to read them, which I don't recommend by the way, I will make you copies before I turn them over to the big guys to be destroyed."

"The phone had pictures on it. Phone numbers for mundane things such as pizza places and Chinese restaurants. All things and places I'd never seen. Then I figured out how to get online with it." Parker thought about how many times he'd used his phone for the same things. To search for something, to order hay or meds for the animals. He'd even bought his house with his phone, putting in the bid and answering the counter bids without ever seeing the house. All things he took for granted. "I found websites about some of the drugs I was forced to take. Then with that I found out that I was a captive, abused by the Internet's standards. I started asking questions, demanding for them to speak to me. Then one day I found a good soul. Reese walked into the building and I could feel her."

"She told me that you came to her, just landed in the front of her cab like you'd been doing it for years. As a hawk at first, then as a clipboard so no one would know you were there, she said." Josh nodded and laughed. "I can almost see her now, trying to act calm while this huge fucking bird sat on the seat next to her."

"She gave me my name. Josh. I don't think she understood at the time what she was giving me with that name. It felt like freedom, like she'd set me free, more than me just getting away." Lauren said she could understand that too. "The man, the one that you were sent to rescue, what ever happened to him?"

"He's dead. Committed suicide about a month after we

got him out." Josh nodded. "He couldn't handle it. Left a note saying that he was still a captive in his head and that it wouldn't go away. What about you, Josh? You still captive? You gonna let these guys rule you?"

"I don't want to." Lauren said that it was up to him. "I don't know what I can do. Nor what I can't do. I'm…they did things to me."

"I'm sure they did. And I'm pretty sure that you're a good deal stronger than they think you are." He said that he was. "Then it's up to you if you let them win or not. Do you crawl into a hole and just let them run over you, or do you get up off your ass and tell them to fuck off?"

Parker was used to Lauren—at least he thought he was—but this was just a boy, and he wanted to tell her to leave him alone. But before he could speak to her, beg her to back off, he felt the difference in Josh immediately.

"I won't let them win." Lauren stood up and so did he and Josh. "Will you help me? I know you can handle things pretty good, but I need control. I have very little of it now."

"I can help you with that. Parker and Reese can as well. Listen to them, Josh. You won't go wrong if you do." Josh said that he would, gladly. "And hang out with his parents. They're a little old fashioned, but about the nicest people you will ever meet. You couldn't do any better than them."

Parker walked out of the station with a lighter step.

He knew that the men out there were coming for Josh. But he knew now that instead of working against them, as he might have done, Josh was going to help them. And Parker knew that they'd only just scratched the surface of whatever else the kid could do. When the men came, they were not going to know what hit them.

~~~

111

Charles sat in his cell and thought of all the things he was going to do when he was released. It was only a matter of time, he knew this. And despite what his former attorney had told him, they would have to let him go once he explained what he'd created. A monster for all times.

"Mr. Dodson?" He said that was his name. "You have a visitor. She said that she's your wife."

"Ah yes, I knew she'd be coming soon. I asked her to bring me some clothing as well as some of my personal things. Could you please make sure that they're set up in here nicely?" The man just stared at him. "And there will be a delivery of furniture as well. Things in here aren't suited to my lifestyle."

"Yeah, about that. Not gonna happen." Charles asked him why not. "Because I don't know if you've realized this or not, but you're in prison. And as such, you don't get to pick what you have in your cell. That's what we're here for. A place where things are tough for you because you've screwed up."

"This is only temporary; we both know that. As soon as I have my conversation with the president, I'm sure he'll make everyone understand that this was just a blip in the road." Charles wasn't insane, but the man looking at him certainly thought he was. It was the look he gave him, like he was eyeing him for a strait jacket. "There will be things going on that you're not going to believe. And as a matter of fact, well above your pay grade. You just don't have the vision that I do. But you'll learn. Perhaps we should have a picture made of us together. No one will believe you when you tell them that you once had me in a cell. And you'll be saying in a few weeks, 'I took care of that man.'"

"It's not really a thrill to be taking care of you. And trust me, Mr. Dodson, it's something I'm gonna remember for a long time." There was censure there. He wasn't sure if the man was trying to hurt his feelings or not. "Now, about your wife. I'm to tell you that there is no screaming at her, no trying to force the glass, nor are you to try to send her any sort of code. If we catch you doing any of these things the meeting will be terminated."

"Glass? I suppose that will be necessary so that you can watch us. But I assure you, there won't be any hanky-panky between us. We've come to the decision in our life that sex between us is not all that satisfying." He was going to be honest with this man, as he expected honesty back. The officer said something like you don't say, but Charles didn't care. He and his wife had an understanding.

Charles gave her money and freedom, and she held onto his arm when there were functions that he was required to go to. And she was discreet. That was the most important thing. And he was as well when he took a lover. He didn't want a scandal, nor did he want anyone snooping around in his closet that might hold it over his head.

When he was led into a room with several other men in the same bright suits, he wondered why they'd be going this route. He looked around when the man told him to go to seat three, and as he headed there, he saw his wife on the other side of a tall glass. Charles was confused and turned to one of the guards.

"I think there has been a mistake. My wife and I can't have a private conversation with all these people around. Not to mention with a wall between us we can't even speak at all. I think you should take her to the correct room." The guard just stared at him. "Come come now, you can't be serious about this. How am I like these people here?"

"You either sit at seat three or we take you back to your

room." Charles asked if his things were there yet. "Things? We never touched your things. Either sit or we go back, up to you."

Charles didn't like this, but knew that if he didn't get this straightened out soon, that things were not going to go as planned. He had a list to give his wife. People to call, and what he needed for her to bring with her tomorrow when she came to see him. Picking up the phone that rang when she picked up hers, he asked her if she believed this.

"What I don't believe is that you're in here. What were you thinking, getting yourself arrested like this? And I can't do this all the time, Charles. They searched me. Dumped out my purse and made me empty all my pockets. Like I was some sort of criminal. I do not like this." He told her that it would be over soon. "I hope so. Also, they told me that I couldn't bring you any clothing unless you were having a court appearance. Your razor and cologne were sent back too. I had to take it all back to the car before they'd let me talk to you. This is just ridiculous. Either fix this or I can't come here again. It's humiliating."

"They can't do that. They can't deny a man his things." He turned to ask about his list and was told that if he was finished that he'd go back. "I'm not done here. I demand to speak to someone in charge. My things were not allowed to be brought to me."

When no one seemed inclined to do his bidding he turned to Alisha again. She was crying now, fat tears that she only let go when she was really upset. He wanted to comfort her, to tell her that it would be all right, but right now he was too angry to say anything.

"Charles, they said you'd be here for a long time. Like years and years. What am I supposed to do if you're in here?

The neighbors are already started to snub me. And I was asked not to return to the club, a place where I was queen. They're treating us like we've done something horrible, and I hate this." He told her it would be over soon. "I hope so. All my credit cards have been cut off. And the things that I put on hold at two of my favorite stores have been put back on the shelves. They called me, told me that the money I put on those things, my things, was no good. Charles, I have to look good, and you know it."

"I know, I know. I'll get to the bottom of this. Did you bring me money at least?" She told him that the bank wasn't releasing any of their funds for any reason. "I don't understand why they're doing this. They're acting like I'm some sort of bad guy. They have no idea.... I'll get to the bottom of this. Just as soon as I speak to the president. I know that he's not the one we supported or voted for, but he's all we have at the moment."

He did his best to calm his wife, but he was upset himself. No matter how many times he told her that he'd take care of it, there was the niggling of doubt that he could. He kept thinking of the people that he'd talked to this morning, and their questions about someone named Josh Savage. He'd told them several times that he didn't know anyone by that name. He had been thinking of the name all afternoon and still had no idea who it might be.

Charles looked at his wife, thinking she might know who it was. "Do we know a man by the name of Savage?" She asked him if it was the person from the lab. "No. I don't know a person there named Savage either."

"Not Savage. But something like that. Charles, what am I going to do about having no money? I can't go out to lunch with my friends and pick up the tab. The credit cards are useless to me if the shops I try to use them in cut them up. That man who did it this morning just pulled out those big scissors like —"

"Savage." She just stared at him. "Not Savage, but SA-8. Good heavens. They want me to tell him where he is so they can take credit for his creation. They might be able too if I can't get out of here. I need to get out of here, Alisha. I need to find him and bring him before the president so I can claim him. I need for you to find me a lawyer, a good one. The best that money can buy."

"How are you going to do that when I can't even bring you a nice pair of your boxers? Charles, you're just not thinking things through here. I'm not getting any money." He told her she'd be fine and got up and left her there.

As he was taken back to his little cell, he thought of the last time he'd seen SA-8. He was powerful, and was going to make him a great deal of money and prestige. Charles was sitting on his bed when he realized that he'd forgotten to ask about his phone. These people were making him forgetful, and he wasn't happy about it. Glancing at the clock that was in the hall, he saw that it was close to dinner time. Good, he'd just get them to bring him one then.

Since they wouldn't give him any paper or pens, he had to try and remember all the things he wanted to say to the president. The man was doing a bad job of running the country as far as he could see. He was nothing like his good friend Joe Irving. He'd read somewhere that he was going on trial soon. Poor man. To be targeted like that by his own men.

Dinner time came and went. He was just ready to yell for someone to come to him when he heard the door down the hall open and close. Finally. Charles went over the ten things on his mental list again just as a woman, a very beautiful

116

woman, stood in front of his cell.

"Can I help you?" The woman only stared at him. "I don't know who you are, but I'm awaiting my cell phone and dinner. If you'd see your way to having them brought to me, I'd appreciate it."

"You're not getting a phone. And your dinner has been delayed because of me." He asked what authority she had to do that. "I'm the woman that says you can't have your dinner until I say so, that's who I am. Christ, the things I do for her. You're a major pain in the ass, did you know that? I could be, right now, fucking my mate, but instead I'm here to take care of you."

"Now see here, I know my rights. And I want my dinner brought to me. It's not very good and your chef could use some pointers, but it's all I'm allowed to have." The woman took a step to the cell door and Charles backed away. "What do you think you're doing? Back up right now before I call someone here."

"I've been sent here to make sure you back off. It might be a little easier than I thought it would be now that I know you. I told her that you didn't have any, not if the things I'd heard about you are even half true. Worth, I mean. A man like you who would try and kill a woman and a kid just can't have anything redeeming about him. Yet here I am, talking to you. Can you be turned around, listen to me when I tell you to back off? I fucking hope so." Charles lifted his chin, not liking at all where this was going. "You will leave them alone or you'll die. It's as simple as that, really."

"What woman? I don't know any kids. What are you talking about?" The woman took another step, then another until she was right up against the bars. Then just like that, she was through them, as if they were never there. When he felt himself being lifted up, a strong hand at his throat, Charles felt his bladder let go and urine run down his leg. "Don't kill me."

"I have been told that I can't. Not yet at any rate. Doesn't mean that I won't taste you a bit. Just to keep tabs on you." Charles felt a slight pinch to his throat, then the woman smiled at him. He saw her teeth then; a vampire. When he was set down on the floor again the woman took a step back. Then she took her fingers to her mouth, stained with his blood. "Stay away from Savage or I will return. And nothing will stop me from making you pay." Then she was gone.

Charles sat down on the floor, unmindful of the urine that he'd spilled. He saw in his mind what she would do to him if he fucked up. All of it just before she disappeared. The look in her eyes, the dark redness of them, made him think that the woman meant business and would stop at nothing to kill him.

Charles sat there when his dinner was brought and then taken away untouched. He was going to stay as far from Savage as he could. No matter what the benefits that he might have gotten from saying he was his creator. He knew the meaning of torture, and she would kill him now if given the opportunity to do so. He even saw the way he would die if she found him alone.

Yes, he thought, I'm going to stay as far from the young boy as I can. No matter what kind of money or fame he could have gotten from talking about him, it suddenly just wasn't worth it.

# CHAPTER 9

Parker thought that in another two weeks he'd be able to harvest his wheat. What he was going to do with it then was anyone's guess. The delay of the dryer and grinder was holding him up in a lot of ways. When he saw Josh coming toward him, he had to smile. The kid was taking to farming very well. He just hoped he would continue to enjoy it come planting season next spring.

"Did you know that there are several different kinds of trout, and that they're related to the salmon and char?" Parker said that he did know that. "But did you know that once you seed a pond with trout you have to fish in it at least once a week?"

Parker started to tell him that wasn't true when he saw the smile. "You've been talking to my dad, haven't you? You do know that he's playing you, right?

"Yes. He is what Reese would call full of malarkey. I think he's funny. Your mom said to tell you that should I get to go fishing with the old coot. And that you were to make sure that Reese didn't give him too much in the way of sweets." Parker

119

KATHI S. BARTON

nodded. "And I'm to ask you if I need to get gear or do you have some. Is there specialty clothing to wear when fishing?"

"He meant fishing equipment. And I have some. It's in the barn." Josh nodded but didn't say anything more. Parker had come to enjoy the time they spent together out in the fields. The kid was smart and had a good head on his shoulders. "I'm guessing that you and Dad have plans for some time soon?"

"Yes, in the morning if you don't mind." Parker said he didn't and for him to have fun. "I have something I'd like to talk over with you. If you have time."

"I have all the time in the world for you." Josh nodded but was still distracted. "Reese is making us steaks for dinner, and Brussel sprouts. I don't care for them usually, but she's doctoring them up with bacon for me."

"If bacon can't fix something, then it's not worth spit." Again, a quote from his dad. He was pretty sure that his dad had borrowed it from someone else, but he didn't care. "I'd like for you to adopt me. And let me be called Josh McCullough."

Parker let out a breath slowly. He wanted to make sure of two things before he answered him. But before he could ask him about either of them, Josh started pacing back and forth and seemingly talking to himself.

"You can't just blurt things out like that, Savage. What if it's not timed correctly? Maybe he had things on his own mind and you messed them up for him. What—?" Parker said his name. "I'm working through it."

"I can see that. Reese does the same thing. Are you sure about this? I mean, me adopting you? And so you know, my family and I have already adopted you in our hearts." He nodded. "I'm going to marry Reese soon too. She'll be your mom if we go through with this. Not that she's not done a pretty good job of it already, but it would have to be both of us to make it work. You don't have to call me Dad if you don't want, but it's something I'd like for you to think about."

"I think that calling you Dad would be wonderful. I haven't talked to Reese yet, but she's already like a mom to me, like you said. I think that asking her would be emotional, don't you?" Parker said it was for him as well. "I'm not human, but then neither are you. I'm different, but I don't think that bothers you too much. And like you said, your parents seem to like me. And your brothers are amazing. Lauren is.... Well, she's nice when you catch her in a good mood, and intense when you don't."

"That about sums her up." Josh grinned. "I'd be honored to adopt you. And to have you called a McCullough. We'll have to talk to Reese, you know. She is…well, she's been your guardian for a while now, and it's only right."

"Yes. I can see that." He nodded. Parker had a feeling there was more, so he bent to check the soil. He didn't need to, but he did it to give the kid time. "I'd like to go to school. I'm pretty smart, but I'd like to go and be with people my own age."

"That would be a nursing home, if you're talking intelligence." Josh laughed. "What sort of education have you had? I'm assuming that they did give you some classes in the lab."

"I was given books to read after a while. Mostly they were books on physics and math. I did get to read some of the history books they had, but I don't think they were up to date." Parker asked why he thought that. "They were talking about putting a man on the moon."

"I believe they have done that, yes." They both laughed again. "All right. I guess you'd have to be tested. I don't know much about how they go about figuring out what sort of class you'd start in or anything. But we can look into it. We'll have to have a reason for you coming here and needing this test. I mean, we can't say that you have records at another school. They'll check that out."

As they made their way to the paddock to feed and take care of the horse, neither of them talked about much but the jobs at hand. It was relaxing in a man to man sort of way. Josh was extremely interested in every aspect of the jobs, and seemed to like it when Parker gave him not only answers to his queries, but also background on why he did things a certain way.

They were headed to the barn when a car pulled in the drive. He told Josh to leave when he didn't know the car.

"Can I help you?" The man got out of the car and watched Josh as he flew away as a large hawk. "Excuse me? Can I help you?"

"We're looking for him." Parker didn't even bother turning to look at the young man. He knew that the man hadn't seen him; Josh had shifted inside the barn. "Can you call him back here?"

"I have no idea what you might be talking about." The man looked at him then, and Parker felt his cat move along his skin. "I think it's about time you turned around and left here. I'll have my wife call the police if you don't get the hell out of here now."

"I think you'll want me to stick around for a little while longer. I have someone that might be able to shed some light on what's going on with the boy. There are people looking for him, and we'd like to help you with that. While I can't get to the one in the underground place, he won't fare so well once he's out. I've been ordered to destroy him." Parker said nothing. The man was well informed, but that didn't mean he

122

was a friendly, as Lauren might call him. "You're not going to trust me with this, are you?"

Parker saw Josh come back. He flew low over the car then landed on the fence post just to his left. Then he saw both Bear and Reese come out of the house. Behind them were the men onsite finishing the work in the kitchen and dining room. Parker didn't feel any safer with them all there, but he didn't let the man see that. He was afraid for them all, if he was honest with himself.

When the door to the back seat of the car opened, Parker watched the beautiful woman get out. Grace was all he could think about. This woman exuded grace and beauty. When she closed the door and walked to him, Josh landed in front of him and shifted to a large bear. The woman stopped moving.

"I haven't come here to hurt any of you. I have my reasons, but to hurt you isn't one of them." Parker said nothing. If he had anything to say, it was cut off when the woman spoke again. The situation was about to go full out shit in about two seconds. "My name is Arial. I've no last name if you wish to try and find me. You won't. I don't exist in any public records. At one time I was called Female-10."

"Parker?" He didn't turn to look at the source of the voice to his left. He hadn't realized that Lauren was around, but when she laughed a little, he did turn. "This is Josh's mother. Or so I think. The paperwork from the lab, it only referred to her as Female-10. No picture or other information other than that."

"How do we know she's not been sent here by the shits that want him?" The man in the front of the car laughed. "You think this is funny? You're not touching my son. Only over my dead body. I'm about ready to tell these people here to attack you both. What the fuck do you think is going to happen then?"

"I knew that to give birth to him in such a place would cause him harm. And since he wasn't what I was, even though he was of my blood, I could not take him with me when I left." Parker asked her why she stayed in the first place. "I had no choice. The iron kept me in place. They had me shackled like I was in a prison even though I had what they wanted most. That child."

Things that he'd read in the file were starting to fall into place. The notes that Lauren had given him had said just a day or so before Josh was born, the chains that held the female had been removed. There had been mention of swelling and bleeding. It also said that the baby had been left swaddled in a blanket, one that hadn't been put in the cell in the first place.

"I brought it." Parker looked at the man. "I couldn't take him either. My job was to care for her and none other. The child was of her body, but it wasn't fully witch. Not that anyone is as strong as her, but there wasn't any reason to take the babe when she'd been so ill. Besides, we both knew that they'd care for the kid, and once she was strong enough, we were going to go back and get him. He is her child."

The shift from bear to Josh was quick. He hadn't moved, not once since the woman started speaking. But now Josh came to him, stood with him and Reese as the man leaned against the car. Arial smiled at them, but Parker still wasn't convinced that what these people were saying was true.

"When he came for me, he knew that I was weak. Weak not just from the birth of the child here, but from the iron coursing through my blood. On the outside, my death, had it occurred, would have meant the death of my child as well. No one would have cared for him where I had gone, and I knew that he was safer in the lab." Parker asked her why. "Because he was all they wanted. A child that could be stronger than any human born, as well as magical. I didn't think, and I still don't, that they meant him any harm. But since I had fulfilled my duty to them, they would have killed me without any hesitation. You see, I could read their minds."

The implications of what she was saying made him think she was full of shit. If she would have stayed or even taken her child with her, then why wait until now to come back for him? And how had they found Josh? She'd not come back for him, neither of them had. And he wanted to know why.

"He was there for eleven years. There wasn't any time for you to go back for him? Send one of your flunkies?" She just looked at the man who had come with her. "He said that he had orders to kill someone. Why have you waited until now to set things to rights? Didn't you realize at some point that they'd do tests on him? Treat him like they did you? Why didn't he go back and kill them all, before this shit happened to Josh, and been done with it?"

"He was lost to me." He asked her how that was possible. "I told you, he wasn't like me. But what you don't understand is, he's more than I am. More than even I could have imagined when they did those things to us. And once I was stronger—a full five years had gone by before I was—he was in a place that I could not breech. They put him in a place that I could not talk to him or go to him. To me…well, I thought him dead."

"I was in a cell. Not like a cage, though there was one of those in the room with me, but in a large dome like cell that was solid. I never really thought of it before, but I think it was made of some kind of steel. Perhaps iron too." Arial nodded and smiled at Josh. But he, like Parker, wasn't having any of it as yet. "I escaped four years ago. My friend Reese got me out of that place by hiding me away. Keeping me safe when I was still a babe in the understanding of the world not known to me. Four years. You could have found me then."

"The men following you, what do you think they would have done had I come to you?" Josh said nothing, but his body was stiff with anger or fear—Parker couldn't tell which—when he leaned against him. "They would have killed us both. But you were never far from my thoughts. I kept you both as safe as I could. Ryan, he's been your keeper since the day you were set free."

"The money." Everyone turned to Reese when she spoke. "The money that showed up at the front desk of the restaurant where I was working. There was the slot machine I won at the little store in Nevada. All money that kept us fed, kept us moving."

"Yes." Ryan laughed then. "You missed some a few times. Or simply left it behind. I was never sure. But after the last few days, I think it was simply that you did not trust that it wasn't from the other people."

"I still don't trust you." Ryan laughed and bent at the waist in a bow. "What's this all about? Why are you here? Why now?"

"They're coming." Parker said they knew that. "What I meant was, it's not just the men from the lab. There are many more that would wish to take this boy. Men who would use him for their own personal gain."

"You mean as a weapon?" Arial nodded at Josh's question. "I can take care of them. I know I've had troubles before with control, but I won't hesitate for a moment to take them out should they come here."

"As it should be. But with my power combined with yours, they'll stop coming here altogether." Parker asked her how that was possible. "Because I'm going to work with him, if you'll allow it. I'll combine my magic with his. We'll be beyond powerful."

~~~

Fritz couldn't stand it any longer. He was sick of his own company, and worse yet, he was hungry. There was nothing left for him to eat, not a scrap of food in the entire compound to have for even a tasty snack. Somehow all of it had simply gone bad overnight.

He'd opened a can of tuna and had nearly fallen over when the stench hit his nose. Christ, it was like a rotten corpse had been put in the tiny can. It had taken him nearly three hours of running the venting system before he could stand to take the wet towel off his face. And even longer still before he thought he could eat.

The second thing he'd opened had been a box of crackers. There was some cheese in the big refrigerator but it had gone moldy. After carefully cutting away all the green fuzz, he'd opened the crackers, only to find them infested with hundreds of little flying bugs. He still wasn't sure what they were, but they'd left their droppings all over the bag and even in the box. He could see where they nibbled, just enough to show on each cracker. He'd ended up throwing out six boxes of the things before just giving up and tossing out every box of crackers he had.

The canned hams that he'd packed away were wormy. Unopened cans of pasta dishes had a green film over them, making them look like pesto rather than creamy alfredo. Each thing he opened, every item that he'd pulled from his pantry, was bad, the expiration dates on each one of them still years away. And now, five full days later with nothing but water to fill his belly, he was ready to eat anything.

"Fucking companies are going to hear from me." What

they might hear from him was still a mystery. He couldn't very well say that they'd sold him bad food that he'd hidden in his hidey hole so that the government wouldn't bother him for crimes he'd committed against them. Fritz thought of the woman then.

She was never far from his thoughts lately. He had no idea why, but he was sure she had something to do with his current predicament. No food, very little water, and his trash compactor and incinerator hadn't been working properly. Not only was he starving, but his home smelled like a trash dump on the hottest day of the fucking year.

Why hadn't she come down to get him? He knew that she had the combination to get down to his level. Every day for a week after he'd spoken to her, he'd sat in his locked bedroom with only himself as company, his gun across his lap, his eyes on the door, waiting for her to come. Fritz wasn't sure who he had planned to use it on, her or himself, but he was ready.

But she'd never shown. No men had come storming into his little home. There had been no men screaming at him to drop his weapon, to get on his knees. Fritz had been so terrified that first day that he'd nearly wet himself several times an hour when the air handler had kicked in, sure it was them coming to get him.

Then as the days started to pass and nothing happened, he began to think that she was playing with him. He still thought—knew, actually—that at any moment she was going to come busting through the door. But he was less concerned about what she'd do with him than he was about what kind of food he could get when he was free. Because he was now a prisoner, the same as if she'd come here and locked him away.

Standing by the door that would both free him and get him locked up, Fritz thought about what would be greeting him on the other side. A squad of armed men for sure. And more than likely a group of men tearing apart his lab. He thought he hated that most of all.

He wasn't going to die if he was sent to prison. At most they would want him to explain his notes, go over what he'd been doing. He might even get to play some in a big government lab, this one regulated more than his had ever been. Fritz also thought that they'd have millions of questions for him. Things he more than likely wouldn't have an answer for. More still that he'd not answer. Some of his answers, he knew, would get him the chair. Even if they didn't use it anymore.

While he'd been in charge of the lab, knew what they were doing and had some input, Fritz wasn't a scientist at all. Yes, he'd graduated from the most Ivy League college that he could find. But it was only on paper; his grades were more or less manufactured, at great cost to himself and his family. He'd never attended classes on a regular basis, hadn't taken any kind of exams, and he'd never been inducted into a fraternity. All lies, all stories that he'd made up from bits and pieces of movies he'd seen, as well as accounts of his colleagues that had actually gone to college.

Fritz had attended college in the sense that he'd gone to the dorm he'd been assigned to, but had never done a damned thing after that. As far as going to classes, he wouldn't even had been able to tell you where the buildings were; nor, for that matter, who might have taught the classes. He'd attended a few at first, but when he figured out he could drink his way through the years, getting into the college records had been far easier than he'd hoped for. It had been expensive but well worth the kudo's he'd gotten from colleagues that were well above him in the scale of education. Once he was out, getting a job had been simple too. A few tweets to his resume had him doing things he'd had to look up to make sure he could lie his way through the interview when asked.

He was, in a word, a fake. Smiling, he thought of what he'd had on his resume when he'd gone to talk to a few investors. The first man had gone over his record with a fine toothed comb, and had nearly tripped Fritz up when he'd asked questions about the process. His answer, he knew, had been less than satisfactory, but he'd fumbled around enough, played the bumbling lab professor enough, that the guy had bought it. Charles Dodson had been their biggest investor, as well as considering himself a part of the team. If he only knew what the monies that had been given to him had gone for. The compound he was in now was a big part of it.

"Fat lot of good the money has done for me when I can't even get a decent meal or take a good crap for all the problems this place has given me." The plumbing had started backing up just that morning. Now not only did he have rubbish all over the place he could do nothing with, the toilet was starting to resemble one of those outhouses he'd seen in rural areas where he'd grown up. "I have to get out of here now, before in a million years they find my body here among the ruins."

Fritz put his hand on the door. He was thinking of all the shit that could go wrong, but his belly rumbled then and he punched in the code. Before the door was fully open, sliding back silently on its mechanism, he knew this was the right thing to do. The smell of fresh air had him dizzy with excitement.

There was no one in the long hall. Not a soul was there with guns or otherwise to meet him. As he made his way up the long stairs that had brought him down to this place, he thought perhaps they would be there, at the top. As soon as he breeched the second door, the hidden one in his office, he giggled.

It was very unmanly, he supposed, a grown man giggling like a child. But he was happy to see no one. Not one single person waiting for him to come out. And better than that, he didn't hear a single sound coming from any part of the lab.

Bypassing the desk — he wasn't stupid enough to try and bring up any of the cameras just yet — he made his way to his other safe. Besides, he'd just noticed that his computer was missing, as well as all his file cabinets were open. It looked as if they'd ransacked his entire office. And for what? Fritz kept nothing in here but some stashes of food, a few bottles of wine, as well as some porn he'd picked up cheap online.

He knew this safe was going to get him to freedom, as well as a good meal and a much needed shower. Pulling the rug up from the floor, he saw that no one had touched it; the dust on the thing looked like it had been there for years. Pressing the buttons to open it up, he looked around again to see what they might have missed. There didn't appear to be anything.

As soon as he had his passport, money, as well as keys to a car he had stashed away, Fritz loaded it all in a trash bag that had been left behind. He had a long way to go to get to his car, and he wasn't going to waste time going through the lab and looking at what was surely a mess. He knew as surely as he was there that nothing was left of it.

When he was in the bright sunlight, he tilted his head back, letting the sun shine on his face. When he thought that he'd give just about anything right now for a thick juicy steak, he made his way across the parking lot to where his car had been parked all those weeks ago. Not only was it still there, but it looked as if someone had moved it for him. It was now closer to the door.

"Someone is watching out for me, it seems." He was

whistling when he opened the door. And when he was inside, he started laughing. "This has got to be the easiest escape anyone has ever done. Not that I've had to escape all that much, but I'm betting this one rates right up there with ease."

Backing out of the space that had been provided for him by some unknown person, he made his way to his first of many stops before leaving town. He was thinking of ways he could get back into creating again even as he turned in the drive to the cemetery. Fritz was going to be nasty rich and free in about four hours. His first stop was going to be a secondary stash he'd made. Cash and jewels were going to be his ticket out of this country.

# CHAPTER 10

Reese was putting the last of the pies in a big box that was going to the shelter when she realized she was making some progress in cleaning things up. Her nerves were frayed right now, but she was making herself do one project at a time and then marking it off the list she'd made. It was the only way that she felt she could cope. Otherwise, she had no idea what she might do.

"Have you given it any thought?" Shaking her head at Bea, she didn't even turn to look at her. She'd shown up a couple of hours ago with not just boxes, but someone to help Reese with the cleanup. "It's not on the market as yet. I don't think it'll be on there long once it is. And you don't have to make sandwiches and such. You could make a fortune in just these baked goods alone."

"That's not on my list right now. I'm dealing with this one before I make another one. One list at a time, if you please." When Bea laughed, she turned to look at her. "I'm sorry, but I'm a little…well, I'm a lot overwhelmed at the moment. I'm going to follow my list until I can get my mind wrapped

133

around everything that is going on."

"You think that might be in the next century?" Reese told her she wasn't funny. "No, I'm not trying to be. But if you think about the length of your list and how few things you've marked off it, you can understand my questioning your ability of getting it done anytime soon."

She did glance down at the list, then at the boxes she had yet to pack up. There were at least seventy things on her list, and some of them were baking items yet to be done. Baking had been a way for her to cope with stress. Over the last few days she'd been dealing with things in just that manner. And now she had to get rid of all the sweets or they would go to waste.

"I'm taking them to the shelter on my way to the funeral home later this afternoon. I'm going to help May see to Margaret's arrangements. See? It's on my list." Bea said that they'd all be in a sugar coma if they ate only half. But she could help her with getting the things taken to the shelter. "I don't care what happens to it so long as it's not tossed out. That would stress me more."

She saw two of the McCullough men come into the room and leave with boxes. Reese had no idea where the boxes had come from or who had put them together for her. There were still three tall stacks of them in the pantry. When Boyd asked if he could take a pie or two home with him, she told him fine. The sooner things were back to normal in here, the sooner she could.... Well, she wasn't sure what she'd do. But she was striving for normal.

Once all the pastries and cookies were gone, she started setting the kitchen to rights. Empty sugar and flour bags were all over. Sprinkles and nonpareils were in spots around the room in the oddest places. Loading things into the sink to be washed, she noticed that not only was Bea helping, but Lauren was in the kitchen as well, sitting at the table with a cup of tea and a plate of berry scones in front of her. Both were untouched. Reese leaned against the sink while the basin filled up with hot soapy water.

"You have any more information for me, I don't want to hear it. If you do tell me anyway, then I'm going to cut you and Colin off from ever having anything I bake again. I think that's a good threat; Colin has already sworn that he'd have my children for me should I bake him macaroons once a week." Lauren just smiled at her. "You make me crazy, do you know that? And I'm not even sure that I like you right now."

"You do and I'll tell you why." Before she finished, Lauren got up and made two more cups of tea and put a dozen or so cookies on a large platter. Then before sitting again, she put another two dozen on it and moved herself and the food to the dining room. "Come on then. We'll sort you out if you think that's what you need. Me? I think you just need to chill."

"Chill? You want me to chill? I have news for you, my chilling out is going to get us all killed. I told you, several times as a matter of fact, that someone was coming. And not only did you not heed my words, but you let the fucking bastard that hurt Josh go. I can't chill with that man out there." Lauren said nothing as she sat down at the dining room table with the treats. "I don't like you."

"Yes you do. Now have a seat." She wanted to ignore her. More than that, she wanted to punch her in the face. Repeatedly. But she sat. Bea told them that she'd be there in a moment and Reese heard the water turn off. "Now. I did let Henderson go because he's not the one we want. He's a part of it, but not the guy in charge."

135

"You said that Dodson was the one financing the project." Lauren said that he was, partly. But only one of them. "Then I don't understand what you're talking about."

"Dodson supplied some money. He gave a great deal to the project, yes, but we have millions of dollars unaccounted for. I don't mean that we don't know where it was spent. Henderson made it his life's work to spend the capitol almost as fast as it came in. We know that Henderson used a lot of the money for the bunker that he was in until recently. He bought houses, boats. Took long trips and stashed a bunch of the cash here and there. All of which we've been able to locate and mark. But, for every dollar that he took, five more would be pouring into the project. From another source." Reese took two of the cookies and smeared the icing all over her fingers before licking it off. "We also know that the former president had his finger in this. It's been added to the long list of shit that Irving is going to trial for."

Reese had heard about how Irving had been taken down. Also how he'd ended up in prison along with some army guy who had been in on it with the guy. She had a feeling that even though her part had been downplayed a great deal, Lauren had a lot to do with their downfall. Reese also thought, but hadn't asked yet, that Lauren's friend Tony had had a major role in it as well.

"And this part with this woman, the one that came here the other day. What do you know about her? And trust me when I tell you, she's not going to hurt Josh. Not so long as I'm alive, she won't." Lauren said she thought she was legit. "As in she's his mom?"

"Yes. While not very complete when it comes to her, she knows more about what is written on the paperwork than a person who hadn't been there would know. For instance, she has said which cell she was in, and knew the names of the other women there. She is also helping us find the other people that might be like Josh. There are other people in the lab somewhere, and we need to find them." Reese asked her why she thought they were still in the lab. "Because it's in the notes. I know that sounds sort of stupid, but it's all we have to go on. And everything else that is there has been checked out as well and has turned out to be right. Like the money in the floor safe that Henderson had. We've taken care that he won't get far with it, played with it a bit you might say. And in the event that he does get out of our reach a little, there is enough shit tracking him that we know just where he is at all times. He takes a shit, we know the color, smell, and texture of it. As for Ariel, I don't trust her. And you shouldn't either."

"Gross. And I don't trust her. There is something very creepy about her. But back to this money. You doctored the money in the safe so that it's all counterfeit, right? And if someone accepts it, what's to say that they'll even check it out? What if they simply put it in their cash tills and deposit it in the morning?" Lauren laid a twenty-dollar bill in front of her. As soon as she touched it she knew it was a fake. Then she looked at the money. "It's a picture of Margaret instead of the president. How did you do that?"

"I have connections. And so you know, my connections are now yours. But Margaret lost her life in this, and we wanted to put her there because of it. Plus, if no one checks it, as you said, the government is going to reimburse them for their trouble. No one will be hurt by this. At least no one that hasn't had anything to do with this shit. We need to figure out all parties, or we're only cutting the fucking head off the thing and not killing it. It needs to die; you can see that." Laying the money back down, she got up and started unwrapping the china that had been in storage. "I don't suppose you can sit still any more than I can."

"I can't think sitting down. I have to be moving." Lauren said she could understand that. "Okay, so Henderson is out, he's got this fake money to burn, and you think somehow that's going to lead you to this other money guy? I don't understand how even your mind raced to that."

"Whoever this money guy is, he's going to want to keep his name out of it. Right now all we have about him is his initial. We have a few names that we think might be a part of it, but not enough to go door to door to check. Whoever he is, he's going to want to be as far from this as possible when it all comes out. Even if he has to kill both Henderson and Dodson."

"They all know each other." Lauren said it was a pretty good bet. "Will he try and come after Josh?"

"I don't know. He can try but he'll never get across the property. Arial and her henchmen aren't going to get within a foot of him either. As you said, she's sort of creepy." Reese got all the plates unwrapped and was starting on the bowls when Lauren continued. "I have a plan, one that you're not going to like but I'd like for you to listen. We have to make these people—a lot of people—think that Josh is killed at some point. If they think he's dead and there is enough evidence to verify that he is, then they'll go away. Or most will."

"You're right, I don't like it. I don't want him hurt. But I see where you're going. However, what about those who don't believe him to be dead? What do we do with them? Kill them and bury them in the south pasture and hope that they make better fertilizer than they did humans?" Lauren told her that was fine by her. "Well, it's not fine by me. I don't want anyone buried in the back yard."

"No one does, dear." Bea entered the dining room with a bowl of grapes and strawberries. There was other fruit in there as well, some kiwi and melon. Dumping a bit of it on her plate, she began munching on it rather than any more sweets. The china was ready to go in the beautiful cabinet now, and Bea started doing that as Reese continued.

"And how does one fake a death? Not that I'm saying we should be doing this, but I'm assuming you have done this before." Lauren nodded at her. "I was kidding. Surely you've not done this before."

"Several times, as a matter of fact." Reese just stared at her future sister-in-law with her mouth open. Lauren was very scary, Reese thought. Scarier than some of the people that might be coming here. "We just have to make it look good and provide them with enough witnesses that aren't family to make it seem real. You have to trust me on this one, Reese. I know what I'm doing, and I have people that will help. It will be flawless."

"You have a plan." It wasn't a question, but Lauren answered anyway. Reese wasn't even sure she was going to agree to this, but listened as the details were laid out.

They were sound and well planned. There were even back up plans should something go wrong. People who would play their parts, in a place where there would be more than enough witnesses. And the topper of it all, Josh would be safe; above everything else, that was what was important.

"I know that this is a good way to end this once and for all, but I don't like it. So many things could go wrong. And not just with this plan. The man, Henderson. What if he never goes to this other guy?" Lauren told her that the man would eventually find Henderson, with her help. "Do I even want to know?"

"I don't think you do, no. But I'd tell you if you asked me." Reese told her she would think on it. "Suit yourself. But know this; you're family now, you and Josh, and so help me, we'll do everything within our power to keep you both safe. But you need to know that this plan, no one can know about it. Not even Parker or Rich. It's important to this plan that there are enough people mourning him that it is real. Understand?"

"You mean lie to him." Lauren said it wasn't lying but just keeping her friend and son safe. "Parker will hate me when he finds out."

"No, he won't. He'll be hurt, yes. I would be as well. But when this is done, and it will be soon, I'll make sure that he understands what had to happen. And the only reason you know is because I think you'd go ape shit in trying to save him Josh when this shit hits the fan." Reese was pretty sure she would have too. "Okay, I need to get things rolling on my end. Remember, it's important that we make this look good."

As she made her way to the door, Reese called her back. "I don't want you hurt either. No one. And while I know that you're doing this to keep us safe, I want you to promise me that you'll be safe as well. I might not like you most of the time, but I don't want you hurt either."

"You love me and you know it. And I promise you, we're working on this so that no one gets hurt but the bad guys. And once they're dead, and they will be, you and I will be besties. Whatever the fuck that is." She moved out the door again, but poked her head back around the corner. "Oh yeah, you might want to have Parker convert you."

After she was gone, Reese sat there with a half-eaten bowl of fruit in her hand and a cold cup of tea. Reese looked up when Bea said her name. She was pretty sure she'd said it more than once.

"She wants Parker to change me into a jaguar?" Bea said that it might be for the best. "A cat? She wants me to be a cat too? How hard will that be?"

"It's painful, yes, if that's what you're worried about." Reese shook her head. "Then what is it? I can answer about any question you might have."

"Can he really do that? Change me?" Bea smiled and nodded. "When? Now? I think now would be good. Yes. Now. We should do it now."

Laughing, Bea told her that she'd have to talk to Parker. "Then after that, we'll have to find a time to do it. You'll be down for a few days. Most people are anyway. I think Lauren was only down for about ten or so hours."

"Well, I have to do better than her." Bea laughed again and Reese was embarrassed. "She's very scary, isn't she? And strong. I'd love to be about half of what she is."

"Oh darling, you're just as scary and strong as she is. On some things more so. You just haven't had to prove yourself yet." Bea sat down at the table and started unwrapping the silverware that had been in the box. "We'll have a big party, an outdoor one, when you get this house finished. I, for one, can't wait to see it. And the food? Oh my, we'll have such a grand affair, and we'll have people coming from miles around. Do you like what has been done to your home so far?"

"Oh yes, very much so. And Parker said that there is enough stuff in the barn that we could put in a little house in the back for me to go and bake if I wanted." Bea was still laughing about her making another list as she left. But Reese kept getting sidetracked in her thoughts.

She thought of what she was going to do when she was a cat. The first thing was she was going to lick Parker all over his body. Then she might let him do the same to her. Yes, being a cat was going to be fun. And she'd be dangerous too, she knew it.

~~~

Parker was just finishing up the last of the bales when he saw the big bird flying over his head. He figured it was Josh, so when he landed on the tractor and turned to him, he almost spoke. But before he could, another hawk came to stand beside the first one. Parker stopped the tractor and turned off the engine.

"I'm assuming that neither of you are Josh. SA-8, if that's what you know him by." Both of the hawks only stared at him, neither of them moving from where they were. "I'm a little freaked out right now. So if you could give me a sign that I'm not going to end up with my eyes pecked out like in that old movie, I'd really appreciate it."

The first one flew to the ground beside him and shifted. It wasn't a boy, like he'd thought it would be, but a woman. She was about his age, he thought, in her late twenties, but he wasn't sure about much right now. When she smiled, the second hawk flew down and did the same. This one was a male, about the same age. Parker was a little scared that not only could he not tell they were male and female, but they had fooled him into thinking they were Josh.

"I've seen that movie." Parker nodded. "It's a very bad representation of us, don't you think? I mean, birds in general."

"I can't remember the plot, but I think something happened to make them a little nuts." She nodded. "Who are you and why are you here?"

"My name is June. This is Walter." He told her his name. "We know you. Parker McCullough of the McCullough jamboree. We've come to kill you. And before you think to shift and take us out, we're stronger than you, as well as more

142

cunning."

"Why?" He felt stupid for this question. "I mean, what have I ever done to you? Besides the movie that I watched a long time ago, I don't think we have anything between us. You have no idea of the shit that is going on right now, and to have the two of you just show up out of the blue is making my cat a little tense. So, either make your move or get the fuck off my property."

His cat moved along his skin, making him feel the need to shift. He was in danger, that much was true. But for some reason, Parker thought he could take them both. And because he was stressed, his cat was as well. Parker stretched his neck, the popping of it making the couple in front of him back up. He liked that; his cat did as well. Calming his cat, telling him that they had this, seemed to help. But he still had no idea why they were there to kill him.

"We've been sent by someone that wants you dead. Really, we're to just make people believe you're alive and with us, but we want to kill you." He didn't say anything as Walter continued. "We're shifters, hawks as you know. This person thinks we can take you there, lock you up in one of the cells, then we get to play. With you. He thought of mice to come help us, but said that even when in human form, they'd not be of much help in this situation. So, how do you want to do this? Do you want to be found dead on your tractor? I believe that to be a little overdone. But it's up to you."

Parker reached for his family. All of them. Told them what was going on, who was with him, and that they'd been sent by some unknown male that said they could play with him. Lauren said she was on her way, but her voice, even in his head, sounded strained, like she was royally pissed the fuck off. Reese said she was coming too, and he found that he wanted her there with him more than anything at the moment. He looked at Walter when he asked again how he wanted to be killed. Like they were picking out a china pattern together and just simply could not decide.

"I'd not contact your family if I were you. We don't have time to fuck with them right now. Later for sure, but not now." Parker pulled his cat back. He was ready to pounce and he really wasn't sure from this distance he could get them both. "You should come down here, Parker McCullough. You have a destiny to fulfill."

The big hawk that landed near him squawked loudly. In that moment, Parker knew that it was Josh. And when he landed on the ground near the couple, he went from hawk to bear then to dragon in a heartbeat. The two of them stood back when Josh spread his wings wide.

*Are you harmed?* Parker told Josh that he wasn't, but was relieved that he was there. *They're not right in the head, in case you missed that. And I smell fresh blood. Do you? It's like they've bathed in it.*

*No, but then I didn't smell them at all when they arrived here. It's like my sense of smell has gone haywire.* Josh told him he'd look into that, but didn't move when he got off the tractor to join him. Parker was careful not to get in front of the dragon, but he was close.

Parker spoke to the couple now. "Now, we're going to talk about why you've been sent here to kill me and who the fuck you work for, or I'm going to let my son here have a piece of you."

*I don't actually think that I could eat them, Dad.* It took Parker a few seconds to realize what he'd just been called. *Pay attention, please. This dragon is hard to hold. As I have never really seen one, I'm...I believe that Lauren calls it winging it.*

*You've winged it very well. Scary, yet not overgrown.* Parker looked at the couple who were holding each other tightly. *Thank you, son. I will never forget this moment for as long as I live.*

"Now, we're going to start over. I asked you why are you here and who sent you? Because I don't believe for one moment that you actually believe that you could take me. Christ, even as humans you're not very much of a threat to me." They started talking at the same time. He got some of it but not a great deal. "Stop."

They both shut their mouths with an audible snap. He felt Colin near him, and the rest of his brothers were coming as well. For the first time since the second hawk landed near him, he was beginning to feel better. He told Walter to speak first.

"We were told to come and get you. But since you've called in someone to help you, which I told you not to do, we'll have to leave and regroup. But we will finish what we came for, Parker McCullough. And for taking you then killing you, we'll be rewarded. We might have done it for free, killing is such a pleasure, but the money will be nice as well."

Parker looked at the woman and asked her who had told them this.

"I don't know his name, at least not all of it. I have his scent but he only said his name was Doc. Why do you even care at this point? It's not like you're going to live long enough to have a conversation with him." Colin came out of the woods as his cat. He did not look like he was in the best of humor right now. But the woman continued before he could ask his brother if there was more going on than just dealing with these idiots. "He approached us while we were walking around the abandoned buildings in town. Like he knew what we were."

145

Parker saw the rest of his family coming up behind the couple. The only one that was human was Boyd, and he wasn't holding his cat back very well. He noticed too that he had his bag, more than likely to fix anything that shed blood out here.

*And what did he offer them? Money? I don't believe that, do you? And Christ, tell me that big dragon is Josh. Otherwise, we're pretty much fucked if he's with these two.* Parker told him it was Josh and that he wasn't doing well in holding him and why not. *Tell him that he certainly has my vote on being the perfect dragon.*

He told Josh what his brother said, and he could feel his control strengthen. It occurred to him then that his brothers couldn't speak to Josh like he could, nor did they know him when he shifted. It was another thing he was going to have to figure out. Especially with all this shit going on.

Just as a large SUV pulled up behind them, Parker had the couple go down on their knees. He wasn't sure what other magic they had, so he had them put their hands up on their heads too. Parker had no idea if that would help, but he did feel better when they complied. Lauren and two of her men came near him and to the couple before he could introduce them to everyone. Lauren shot the man in the head and put her gun on the forehead of the woman. No one moved.

"You killed them." He started to ask her who she was talking about when Josh touched his arm. He looked at the young man and stepped back when he pulled him. "You fucking killed them all, and for what reason? Because you were told? I don't fucking believe that any more than I believe this bullshit story about this Doc person."

*There are nine dead and three more in critical condition. These two entered a grocery store about an hour ago and shot everyone that they could see. The only reason the count wasn't higher is because they ran out of ammo. They were looking for you. Trying to get someone to tell them not just where you lived, but where on the ranch you were. They thought taking you would get them Josh and Reese.* He looked over at Colin as he continued. *Lauren was first on scene. She just told me what is going on. I'm sorry, Parker, but had you gone with them, you'd have never come out alive.*

*They were never going to take me anywhere but kill me here. Do you know who sent them?* Colin said he had no idea at this point, but he was sure that Lauren would get it. *Christ, this is a nightmare. This guy, Lauren thinks it was the unknown person, doesn't she? The one funneling money to this project?*

*Yes. She's almost positive. And so you know, these two might only be the first of many coming for you soon. We have no direct way of knowing until we find this bastard.* He looked over at the woman, who was stubbornly trying not to open her mouth.

*She can't get her to talk. But I'm betting that Josh can.* Colin said that she was working hard not to shoot her in the head. *He's got some pretty amazing powers of his own.*

*Will he try?* He turned to Josh and asked him if he could do it. When he nodded, Parker looked back at Colin and told him he would. *Just tell him to be careful. Whoever is funding this shit, we think he might have his own bit of magic. Maybe not his own, but someone is helping him, we think.*

As soon as Josh walked up to the woman, Lauren moved to the side. Her gun was still on her forehead, but she let Josh take the lead. Instead of talking to her, as Parker was pretty sure that they all thought was going to happen, Josh put his hand on her head and squeezed.

The woman screamed. Blood began to pour from her nose, but no one stopped Josh. As he stood there, his hand on her head, the woman screamed again, this time with information. And when she collapsed, blood still pouring, from her ears now too, Boyd stepped in but didn't touch her. Parker wondered if he was going to do anything when he looked at Lauren.

"I can tell from here she's gone. I could try something heroic, but to be honest with you, I just don't care. The carnage that they left behind…I can't help her."

No one told him he was wrong. It was the first time in Parker's life that he didn't see his brother go above and beyond what was required of him as a doctor. Whatever his brother had seen there, it had affected him deeply.

"His name is Doc, but it's a nickname. His real name is Ryan Holliday. They were approached by him to do just what they told you. Come here, get you, and do whatever they wanted with your body when they had you. This man, Holliday, he's figured out that Mom and I are staying with you guys. They were paid half, and were to get the other half when I was captured." Josh looked down at the dead woman and man. "They were willing to do this for money. Just money that they didn't really need."

Parker was at a loss for words. He didn't know how to explain greed to someone who had a heart like Josh did. Nor did he know how to tell him that these people were actually the norm, that greed was an accepted way to get things you neither needed nor wanted. Parker felt baldly for his new son.

# CHAPTER 11

Fritz came out of the hotel feeling betrayed. He had been ready to pay for his room with a view, and had been told that his money was no good. Not only was it no good, which he'd had pointed out to him, but it was also illegal to try and use it. He thought he'd convinced them that he'd had no idea. But it had been scary there for a little bit.

All the money that he'd stashed away, all the identifications that he'd had made, were shit. Whoever had found it, and he had no doubt who it had been, had made sure that not only could he not leave the country now, but that he'd have no funds to even take care of his personal needs. The fucking bitch was going to pay for this. He was going to make sure of it.

Fritz was broke, dead broke. Not only that, but his stashed car had been vandalized, his clothing had been cut up, and he had nothing to eat. He wasn't sure what he was going to do about cash and accommodations now. He was also pretty sure that the woman he'd talked to had put some kind of device on his car that had it stalling out every mile or so. Fritz had

149

finally just left it beside the road, too fed up to try and fuck with it anymore.

He looked up the street and saw a man he thought he knew. Ryan Holliday was in town? It bore some more investigating, and Fritz made his way to him. By the time he was about ten yards from the man, he knew that was just who it was. But Fritz wasn't sure if he should approach him.

The man had lost more than most on the fact that the lab had been closed down and their best bet for a return was gone. He'd been leading the man on a merry dance for a few months now, asking for more money for this or that. Even going so far as to tell him that they'd had a second success, which they had not. The lab had been a great money maker for Fritz, but he doubted that Ryan would see how that benefited him.

The man had to know about the lab. Ryan had been there nearly every day for the entire time since SA-8 had been conceived. And he'd sit for hours watching the test subject Female 10-1, like she was going to give him some kind of insider information. Ryan had acted like his money had entitled him to some kind of special treatment. He supposed in a way the man was right. And it had been difficult to move the money around with him there all the time. But Fritz had managed well enough. Fat lot of good it had done him.

Ryan had been a burr in their asses almost as soon as the ink had dried on the first check he'd written them. But they'd been all right with it then; the sheer number of zeros on the check had funded a great many things. Including some really nice toys for himself.

After the building had been renovated with the most up to date equipment, some of which he had no idea what it did, Fritz had taken a little payoff for himself. He thought that he deserved it; he had gone and found the man, hadn't he? So the boat, the car, and the truck to haul them around had been his gift to himself. A perk, Fritz had called it.

Then after that, he'd decided that he needed a place to hide. Not from the people who now hunted him, because... well, frankly, he wasn't afraid of them. But he was terrified that one of the creatures they created would be like The Walking Dead people he'd seen on television once.

So now, instead of going to the man, asking him why he was there, or for help for that matter, he stayed back. Fritz hid in the dark shadows of the empty building. Just as he was ready to turn away from him, hide better, he saw the woman.

She was a beauty, he'd say that for Ryan's taste in women. Her long dark hair did nothing to diminish the pale porcelain-like tone to her skin. But the dark clothing, black from head to toe, was a little creepy, he thought. Fritz knew there were creatures out there that thought that to dress the part of a villain was the way to go—he had no doubt that was what she was for some reason—but he thought it off putting. Then when the two of them started arguing, he got a little closer to listen to them, more careful now of not being seen.

"They're dead? You let them be killed for no reason? Why the hell were they in the store anyway? Did they not think to ask someone before they went into this place and killed a bunch of the stupid citizens? Christ, people will be all over us now. Do you have any idea how hard it was for me to make them homicidal? I mean, they were already insane, but to make them enjoy killing takes a huge amount of magic that wears me out." He'd heard the commotion about someone shooting up a grocery store about three hours ago. Fritz wondered if that was what she was talking about. "All they were to do was get the man, and then the rest would be easy, you said. You lied to me, and now I have to go and figure out how to get closer to them so that I can bring them to us. I told you to wait, damn it."

"Well, I'm sick of waiting. I paid good money for that boy. You have no idea how that galled me to pour out millions and millions of dollars to get nothing. And now he's gone. Just gone, and there isn't anyone I can ask about it. Those Feds have that place so locked down that I don't think even the rats are hanging around anymore. I fucking want what he can do for us. We should have gone in there right then and taken him for our own just like you told me to do all those years ago. I'm sorry. So sorry that I didn't listen to you." The woman paced and the man sounded angrier now. "What do you care about a couple of flunkies anyway? We were going to get rid of them when this was done. Someone just took them out for us, that's all. You already have an in with the family, and they like you, right? They believe you're the long lost mommy of that monster and want you to be a part of their loving family. Sickening, if you ask me."

"I *am* his mother, you moron. And yes, I do have an in with the family. But I'm not sure what they think about me, or even if they trust me really. Someone is blocking their thoughts, and I have a feeling it's my dear soon to be departed son. I would say that it's likely that monster I gave birth to isn't going to be as easy to take as we thought. Lucky for us they don't know what I feel towards him either, but they will soon enough. Christ, when I think what I had to endure all those months closed up in that cell for that thing. You should have gotten me out before he was born, Doc. I begged you for it. Now look. We have to sneak around and try to get him to trust me. Fuck. I told you from the start that we'd have to go back and get him right after I was home. I just knew he was what they were looking for, what we were all looking for.

But you wanted to wait. What reason did you have for that, anyway?" If he answered her, Fritz didn't hear what he said. "Now he's out there, and we're just waiting for him to figure out everything we did to him when I was pregnant. This will end badly if we don't fix it before he gets wind of all this shit, Ryan. We have to fix this or we're fucked. And dead."

Fritz wanted to know what that might have been, what sort of things they'd been up to without his knowledge. The woman had been a controlled subject, her pregnancy monitored daily. The room they'd had her in was temperature controlled. And even though she never ate a bite of it, her meal items were written down when they were taken to her and then taken away. How did they do something that he'd not been aware of? Whatever they'd done to her on their own, he wanted to find out. He watched as they seemed to come to some kind of understanding, but he was still left in the dark.

Then, when he thought them to part ways—Ryan to his hotel that was no doubt the best that could be had, and the woman off to wherever she'd been hiding out—she turned back to Ryan and smiled. The same kind of smile that he'd seen on her face a dozen times when she'd been in his lab.

"Oh yeah, I forgot to ask. You have the book, right? You were able to get it from the lab?" Ryan shook his head, saying that they were still looking for it. The smile went from one he'd come to recognize as you're a fucking bastard to I'm fucking going to kill you in a second. "Damn it, if they have that book and can even understand half of it, then we're not going to have the only monster that came out of that place alive. You did get in and kill those other creatures, didn't you? Please tell me that you did do that at least." Ryan nodded and told her he'd seen to it personally. "Christ, that would have been a disaster had they found them too. But you have to go back and get it, and barring that, the guy who wrote it down. Have you done anything to contact Henderson? Last I heard he'd crawled into a hole and had yet to resurface. What about him?"

"No. I've not seen or heard from him at all. You'd think that he'd at least have the decency to let me know what's going on here. Not that I need him to tell me it's all gone to shit in a creek, but a phone call wouldn't have been remiss. As for the book, it's not there. The safe that he had in his office is empty. And trust me when I tell you, we looked hard. There was a safe in the floor, but it was only filled with stupid shit. Funny money and some ID's that even my own mother would have seen were fake. Christ. I paid all that money to get the combination, and it was for shit." *His safe? His partner had wanted his things from his safe? What kind of deal was that?* he thought. "For all I know, he hid it with him when he crawled away with his tail between his legs. The fucker. But I've been thinking, as soon as we find the book, we can just forget about this kid, right?"

"Are you kidding me? Yes, we're going to keep trying to bring the kid over to our side. Or at the very least, we're going to put him in a cell and hold him. Don't you see, he's the key to everything. The funding that we'll need will be easier to get with him there to do his tricks. The bigger better lab too. We'll even be able to afford the best men working for us. Not to mention the skim that we'll take from them all. No, I've changed my mind about killing him, we need him more than ever. To prove to the world that we're not just fucking around here." The woman turned and looked in Fritz's direction, almost, it seemed to him, as if she knew he was there. "Ryan, do you get the feeling that we're being watched?"

"Watched? No, I don't feel that way. What is it you're

feeling?" Fritz closed his eyes and didn't move. If she knew that he was there and came after him, he didn't want to know what it was she was going to do. "There are a lot of people around us, Ariel, but no one seems to be paying the slightest attention to us."

"I feel it." He asked her again what she felt, and Fritz opened one eye to see what she was doing. Now she was looking down the street from him. "Someone is out there, and I can feel them, I'm telling you."

While keeping an eye on her, Fritz backed up. He knew when he was inside the building again; things were considerably darker in there. But he never took his eyes off the couple right in front him. Fritz had a scary feeling that if either of them caught him here, not only would he be dead, but it wouldn't be an easy soft death either. He'd suffer like no one had before him. And he wasn't ready yet to give up on finding the kid before they did.

Fritz didn't care a fig newton for the other people, but SA-8 had belonged to him. Fritz knew that of the three of them, he was the one who had gone in there every day no matter the weather. He'd had to suffer through answering endless questions from not only Doc, but also Charles. And they had stolen from him.

As soon as the couple moved on, Ariel still looking around for him, he was sure, he let out a long breath. He had to get going, make plans, and the sooner he got started on them, Fritz knew the safer he'd be. He was glad now that he didn't know where his notes were. If he did, then they'd take them from him. Not that he wasn't going to try his best to get them back, but now he had another agenda. To beat them to SA-8 and make the money they were hoping for.

"First and foremost, I have to get some cash." He was still

rankled about how he'd been had over that. Whoever had his cash, he hoped they enjoyed it. "Fuckers. I swear to Christ, when I find that woman, I'm going to make her pay."

While he'd had no doubt it was her, Fritz actually felt his balls tighten up closer to his body. Every time he thought of the woman, whoever she was, his body would do that. There was something so very profoundly scary about her. And he didn't think he was wrong in thinking that. She was one bad ass bitch, and he was going to avoid her as much as he possibly could.

~~~

As quietly as she could, Reese moved along the tree line to hide. She wasn't any good at this stuff—stealth wasn't her bag—but she was enjoying herself. And every time she was able to outsmart Parker, which wasn't often, he told her that he'd give her something special. She didn't care what it was, so long as he loved her forever.

She thought of the funeral and the reading of the will after. May had taken it very hard, and told Reese that she and Margaret had never let a single day go by without talking to each other. Now she wasn't even able to see her, much less talk. It broke her heart. Then she spoke of the diner.

"I can't do it any more, child. Not one bit of it. Every time I go in there, even to have me a cuppa coffee, I just break down. I can't do it." Reese nodded and held Parker's hand as they sat there. "You two buy it. Take it off my hands and run it. You need it more than I do."

"Oh no, you—" Parker squeezed her hand. She looked at him and he just nodded and smiled at her.

"We'll do that, May. But you have to make us a promise. That you'll come by and see us at least once a day. I'm serious. I'll have it put into the contract that you have to visit."

May had agreed, tears flowing down her cheeks as she thanked them both. Reese thought it was the best thing they could have done for the poor woman. And she loved Parker all the more for what he'd done. That had been two days ago, and now they were playing.

*I can see you.* Reese moved her eyes this time when he said that to her instead of stomping her foot and asking him how. His laughter made her think he'd been trying to trick her into coming out of hiding. *You're by the maple tree, on the left side of it. You're currently leaning against it with your arms holding it from behind. And you have a leaf in your hair.*

*Damn it.* He laughed again, and she felt a smile tug at her mouth as she pulled the leaf, which was just where he said it was, from her hair. *You can't be that good.*

*No, I'm not. You're that bad.* Well that sucked. It was the truth but it still sucked. *I love that you're trying. But if you'll let me now, I'll tell you what you did wrong.*

No one wanted to be told how they were screwing up. But she'd been at this for hours, trying her best to outwit someone that could smell a fart from eighty miles. Well, probably not that far, but he could find her without much effort. When she moved out from her crappy hiding place, he was laying on the ground like he'd been just waiting for her to show herself.

*You're very beautiful when you're pissed off.* Reese flipped him off. *Come here and sit by me. I want to touch you.*

She moved to sit on the ground near him. She'd not be able to sit long; the weather was turning colder every day and she wasn't furry like he was. But she didn't mind doing it for a little while. Almost as soon as she was sitting, he put his head on her lap. Reese rubbed him behind the ears as she spoke.

"I'm worried, Parker. It won't be long now before the babies will be born. I'm bringing that up now because of this threat still hanging over us. And while I know that Lauren can take care of them better than most moms would be able to do, it still is scary to know that someone might try and hurt them." Parker agreed with her. "Josh is so excited for our court day tomorrow. I think he's signed his new name at least a couple of dozen times just today. And then the testing for classes is right after."

*The school isn't aware of his background. Did he tell you that he and I worked on one for him?* She told him that she'd heard some of it but not all the details. *We made up a story that his parents are deceased and there were no other relatives that were in a position to take him. Lauren has pulled some strings for us to get him some transcripts that he can use from a teacher that she knows somewhere. He'll still have to dumb down his testing if he wants to remain in a school for his age group, but he's decided to take some online college classes too. I've already purchased him a computer, and we have Internet in the house too.*

"That's good. I had a really old computer in my rig, but we were afraid to use it much, what with us being chased all the time. So how did we end up with him?" He told her. "Do you think that anyone is going to believe that we met his parents by chance one day and that we formed a solid relationship?"

*I don't care if they believe it or not, so long as they don't question him being with us. Or try and take him from us.* She would kill them if anyone tried. *Also, the school that he's applied for, it's run by the local paranormal groups. Once he's made it in, he'll see that while from the surface it's a regular school, on the inside they do things a little differently. We, he and I, thought it would be better if he didn't start out with a lot of humans around. They'd ask questions that we don't have answers for as yet. I wanted to thank you again for letting me take care of this for him. We've had a good time.*

"I think he enjoyed it too. He's been around me for a long

time, and I think he needed some manly time. But this school, like how different? Do I have to worry about someone hurting him when they have a bad day? Parker, I need him to be safe." She felt silly saying that when she knew that if anyone was safe, it was him. He could be a flipping dragon if he needed to be. But Parker spoke before she could tell him her concerns.

*He'll be safer there than anywhere else he could be going. The type of student body alone will give him the security that he won't get from elsewhere. Because no one there is human, he can sort of be himself. To a point. Then there is the added curriculum that will do him a world of good.* She asked him how. *He'll get to know other paranormal, as well as learn a lot about each of them and their bylaws and rules. Because of the lab setting he's aware of other species, but doesn't know a lot about them.*

"Maybe I should enroll too." Parker said he'd teach her whatever she wanted to know. "Thanks. But can you teach me to be more like your mom and sister-in-law? I've never met anyone more organized, or as bat crazy about their family as those two can be. And your mom? Sheesh, she is the best. She's the type of woman that could just tear you apart without raising her voice while she's knitting a pair of booties. Which, by the way, she's really good at too. And she does it with such grace and understanding that you just can't be mad at her when she's done."

*You should have heard her when I was in third grade. This teacher thought that making me stay in class every day while the others went out to play, reading about the monstrous things that she'd heard of in books, would make me less of a jaguar. I have no idea what she thought me reading romance novels would do to me, but I sat there and got an education that my parents were not happy about.* Reese laughed and laid back on the ground to listen. *My mom enjoys a good romance book. I think she might even like the*

159

*bad ones. They're escapism, as she calls them. And while sometimes she will pick apart an author's information about what they're presuming about our kind, she is never mean about it. Nor has she ever gone online to embarrass or hurt someone. I've always thought she should try her hand at writing them. She sure has read enough. But she told me once that while she reads the wonderful stories that come from the minds of creative people, she didn't want to be one. Anyway, sorry, I got sidetracked. I was in the living room one day reading an assignment because of a nasty comment that I gave my teacher. Ms. Graham had asked me if I was going to shift again and I told her I was. Quite often if I could. Needless to say, she was not happy with my answer. This book just happened to be one that my mom had too. They weren't as racy as the books I'd been reading at school, but just as bad in places.*

"I thought when you said monstrous, you meant like horror. What sort of things could she have thought that you reading romance novels might have given you?" He told her. "I see. She figured that sex would turn you off. I wonder if she realized how good you would get at that. But go on, I want to know what your mom did."

*I'm going to eat you when I'm finished, just to prove to you how good I really am.* Her entire body warmed at the thought of him doing just that. *My mom asked me how I came to having one of her books. And I told her, quite innocently as a matter of fact, what the teacher had been trying to get me to do.*

"Oh my." Parker moved over her, his body warming hers in ways she was sure he'd not meant to. Or maybe he had. She didn't know really, nor did she care. "Finish the story, Parker. I want you to do to me what you said."

*Gladly. The next morning, I got up to go to school and found out that mom was going to take me. I was surprised by the change, but excited too. We were going to have a nice breakfast, she told me,*

# PARKER

*before we went to see my teacher. By the time I was headed into my class room, excited to introduce my mom to my classmates, Mom had a full steam of meanness going on and I was blind to it. At least until she walked in the room with me.* Parker nipped at the buttons on her blouse and spit them out while he continued. *I call it meanness because my mother would never be hateful to anyone. Not even narrow minded women like that teacher was. I was both proud and embarrassed that day. But since then, I've come to realize how right my mom was in how she took care of the problem.*

Her body was heated, too hot for the evening cool air blowing over her. Unbuttoning the rest of her blouse, she felt the lick of Parker's tongue over her navel and ribs. Telling him to hurry with the story, she whimpered when he moved to settle between her legs. Sitting up to watch him, she told him again to finish it.

*She went right up to the teacher and slapped her. Not a girly kind, but hard enough to knock the woman back on her ass. When she started to rise up, Mom snarled at her, letting just enough of her cat go to make sure that the teacher saw her.* Take off your bra for me. Doing as he asked, she hurt she needed to come so badly. *Mom told her that if she ever, in all her life, told a shifter or any other paranormal that what they were wasn't good enough or was a monster, she'd hunt her down and tear her apart. And just for good measure, Mom swiped the blood off Ms. Graham's swollen lip and licked it. Then she told her that she would forever be in her thoughts and actions.*

"What happened then?" Parker told her to take off her pants. It was difficult with him there, so close to her, but she managed to peel them off. "Tell me."

*Four days after that incident the teacher disappeared.* She looked at him as she was pulling her socks off too. *She didn't kill her, if that's what you're thinking. But she did scare her enough*

161

*that she not only quit teaching, but she moved to large ranch and became a recluse. I guess to her dying day she was terrified that Mom would come after her. I believe to this day my mom hates that she did that to her, made her turn away from humanity like she did. But she wasn't there to poison any more minds. For years after that, I was worried too much about what people thought of me.*

"Good for your mom. See? I need to be just like her." Parker said she was, but he didn't want to talk about his mom right now. "Oh, okay. You want to eat me, you said. Are you going to, or are you just all talk?"

He nearly threw her back on the ground with a bump of his head. His tongue licked over every inch of her. Her face and belly. Even her feet and toes were soaked by his administrations. But he never touched her where she needed him most. Opening her legs wider to him, she cried out when he nuzzled his big head there and then nipped at her thigh.

"Please, Parker. I need to come hard."

He teased her more, making her breathless one moment and pissed the next. By the time he licked her pussy, she was hurting so badly that she wasn't sure she'd last much longer without killing him. Or at least hurting him a little. The moment he gave her a brief but powerful climax, she knew that he was going to make her pay.

The first real climax came as she was begging him for more. Her entire body bowed up off the ground, the scream of release stuck somewhere between her pussy and her throat. And when he brought her again, pulling her over the edge twice before she was able to breathe again, she did scream out his name as every part of her body came apart.

*Come for me again.* She wanted to tell him she didn't have it in her, that she was done. But he wasn't having anything like that, and his cat fucked her with quick hard strokes of his tongue. If she died right at this moment, they'd find her with a huge smile on her face and her body so relaxed that she'd be a puddle on the ground.

Her body burned with exhaustion. Even her fingers were exhausted from holding onto herself as she came. And still he gave her pleasure. Or torture, she wasn't sure yet. When he moved off her, Reese thought he was finished, but he wasn't; it was Parker's turn. Even as he shifted over her, becoming her Parker, he slammed hard into her sheath, bringing her over the edge again not just once, but lifting her up to the highest peak only to drop her to the ground twice.

"You're mine." She told him she was. "Say it to me, Reese. Tell me that you belong to me and no other."

"I love you. And will for the rest of my life. I belong to you, heart and soul. No one will ever come between us." He kissed her deeply and when he lifted his head, she finished. "I belong to you and no other. Not even death will tear us apart."

He bit her in the throat then, tore at her like he was going to kill her. But she didn't care, her body was ready for him, needed to feel him fill her. And when he lifted his head and threw it back, he roared, his cat running over his skin like he was with them. Reese came, screaming out so hard, so loudly, that she knew she was going to have a sore throat in the morning.

Then Parker was gone, and his cat stood over her, panting. If she'd had the strength, she might have touched him, but he growled low, his body stiff with something she didn't understand. And before she could look around, try to see the danger that they might be in, he bit her, his teeth ripping into her belly quicker than she might have been able to blink.

The pain was excruciating. And when he shook his head

as if he wanted to rip her apart, she screamed again, this time in so much pain that she was sick with it. Parker was speaking to her, saying words that had no meaning to her while she dealt with the overwhelming terror in what was going on. When the big cat lifted his head from her and moved down her body, she thought for sure he was going to leave her there to die. That she'd just had the most incredible sex in her life, and now she was going to rot out here.

Reese heard the bones in her leg snap before the pain took her. Screaming again, not even having the strength to move away or to shove him away, she cried. Warm blood pooled under her. The pain was there but it was so much, so overwhelming that she couldn't even place where it was coming from on her body. Reese simply hurt everywhere. And when she saw Parker's face near hers, she watched the tears fall over his beautiful cheeks as words spilled from his lips.

"I'm so sorry. So sorry, love. I tried to stop him." She tried to ask him who, but her lips didn't work. Reese couldn't even lift her arms to beg for him to hold her. "My cat has started the process of converting you. I know that we talked about it, but I wanted to explain to you first how it would work."

"Change me?" Her body was melting, it felt like. Her legs no longer worked, her hearing was off as well. And even the simple movement of her eyes was painful. "Dying. I'm dying."

"No, you're not going to die, do you hear me? Damn it, Reese. You will not die." She smiled inwardly. She'd die if she damn well wanted to, she thought. "Reese? Reese? Can you hear me?"

She could, she thought, but it was too late. She knew she was dying and there wasn't a thing she could do about it.

Forcing her eyes open again, Reese wanted to tell him that she loved him, but nothing worked, and when her eyes closed, she was sadder still because she didn't get to say the words to him one more time. That she loved him.

# Chapter 12

Colin wasn't sure what he was supposed to do right now. Meeting with the couple's attorney had come out of the blue. He'd called early this morning and said it was important that he and Lauren come to his office.

"My wife is out of town right at the moment. She had some work to do and will be home tomorrow." The lawyer, Colin couldn't remember his name right then, had tisked. Then he asked if Colin would come in. "Sure, but I'm bringing my own lawyer if you don't mind."

"Oh no, that'll be great. Then we can.... Never mind. Just come on in and we'll talk. It's important that it's today." Colin asked him if there was a problem with the babies, and he just laughed. A maniacal laughter that frightened him even more. "Come in and we'll talk."

So here he sat in the office waiting for the attorney — James was his last name, he'd remembered on the way in — while he was on the phone. Colin looked over at the attorney that had come to him an hour ago.

When he'd told Lauren about the call, she said that she'd

167

send someone to go with him. He had an attorney of his own, one that did some of the corporate stuff when he was working, but she told him this guy was the best. What she failed to mention, and he was sort of glad that she had, was that he was also the Jarvis's attorney. The President of the United States had sent his own personal attorney to go with him. Needless to say, Colin was worried about the need of someone so important in this.

"I'm sorry." Colin looked at James and nodded. "It's been a nightmare here since just before I spoke to you. I want to thank you for basically dropping everything and coming in here now. But there are things I need to verbally make you aware of concerning the adoption of the children."

"They're fine? You said they were all right." James nodded. "Then I don't understand. Are Peter and Wendy backing out of the deal?"

"No. They're both ready to move on with their separate lives, apart. No, it's not that." He paused like he was trying hard to gather his thoughts. Colin wanted to get up and hit the man. He wasn't sure if anyone could blame him under the circumstances, but if he didn't get to it soon— "Wendy went to the doctor yesterday morning and they took her over to the hospital. It seems that there was a mistake on the first ultrasound they did. They aren't fraternal twins as we were first told."

Not twins. They'd been planning for a set of twins, a little girl and a boy. He wanted to ask him which they should expect, a girl or boy, but he didn't want to sound callus. So instead of talking to the man, he reached out to Lauren and asked her if she had time to listen to him.

*Yes. I'm sitting in my office here instead of out in the war room seeing what I can do to kick some bastard's ass. What is it?* Colin told her. *Oh. Well, that's not too bad, is it? A single baby? I guess that's better than us not having any children. We can see how badly we fuck up one life before we venture out on more.*

He could feel her disappointment; hell, he was dealing with his own. And the fact that she was trying so hard to be brave, he loved her all the more for it. This would be fine, he knew it. They'd still have a baby soon.

*True. We might really suck at this.* He didn't believe that and he was pretty sure she didn't either. *Well, we have everything we might need if we decide to have another one sometime. And enough diapers for ten more.*

*Yeah, I should have read that quantity better before placing that order. I guess we can be happy that I got the variety pack rather than all of them in newborn.* They had an entire room, a large room, devoted to just boxes and boxes of diapers and wipes. He had to smile every time he thought of the delivery guy's face as he brought them in the house. *I wish I was there with you. Is Devin helping any? I met him once a long time ago. He's a stand-up guy.*

His attorney was looking at him oddly, and he told Laruen he'd talk to her later. When he smiled at Devin, he just shook his head. Laughing, he asked after Lauren. That was when Colin realized they were alone in the room.

"Are we done here?" Devin said they were only just getting started. "I don't understand. Nor do I get why we had to come in here right now. Do you?"

"Yes. You weren't paying attention, were you?" Colin said that he wanted to tell Laruen what was going on. "Yeah, you might have to revise whatever it is you told her, I'm thinking. When did you tune us out?"

"I didn't tune you out. I was merely telling my wife that we were only going to have a single child. I don't suppose you know if it's a girl or boy, do you? Not that it matters, but we

169

could put a plan in place for the room." Devin smiled again. "You know something you feel I should, don't you?"

"Yes. Plenty. And I'm glad that you're sitting down. More glad than you can realize that I get to be the one to break this news to you. The only thing that would make this better is if Lauren were here too. You're not having a single child." Colin was confused and asked him what he meant. "I mean that they did read the ultrasound wrong. You're not have a single boy and a single girl."

"I think you need to explain yourself." Devin laughed, threw back his head and laughed hard. "What's going on here?"

"Wendy isn't having twins. She's having two sets of identical twins. A pair of boys and a pair of girls. The doctor has put her in the hospital and on complete bed— Colin, are you all right? You look slightly green."

His head was between his knees all of a sudden. And for the first time since someone had first done that to him, he was glad to stay right where he was. Shoes; Colin tried to concentrate on the two pair of nice shoes he could see. But the questions that were going through his head wouldn't stop.

"Four? You're saying that four babies are...? We were worried that we'd fuck up one of them as twins. Now we have...I think we're going to be glad for the diapers." Devin asked him if he wanted a drink. "No. I need my wife. I have to...Christ, she's going to shoot someone over this. Maybe not. Maybe she'll be happy. I hope. Four?"

"Yes. Four. So far." He looked at the man, suddenly terrified. "I'm sorry. I couldn't help it. Yes, there are only the four. Two sets of twins. But in your conversation with yourself just now, can I assume that you still want them?"

"Yes." He hadn't talked to Lauren yet, but he was sure

that she would agree. "If we don't take them, they'll end up in the system, won't they?"

"Yes. And if they do get someone to adopt them, they'll more than likely be separated from each other. No one wants to take on four at once, not most people anyway." He told him they would. "I figured as much. And so you know, I've also requested a few things from the parents regarding this new information. There will be some financial help with the children. A trust fund set up for an education for each of them."

"We don't need that. We're just happy to have the babies." Devin said it was for the best. And since they were going to tell the kids they were adopted, it would go a long way in smoothing any hurt they might have when they found out. "Okay, I can see that."

James came back into the room looking a little less stressed than he had before. He supposed the man knew what he was, him being a wolf himself, and had more than likely expected the worse from him. Shifting on his seat, he tried to keep up with what was being said and the paperwork changes when all he could think about was having four children. Lauren asked him if he was all right.

*Better than all right. You're going to be a mommy.* She laughed and told him she knew that. *Well, miss smarty pants, did you know that we're not having one child as I thought, but four?*

There was silence at her end and he had to smile. It wasn't often that he could get the better of Lauren, but he was pretty sure that he had now. And when she started cursing quite loudly in his head, he leaned back in the chair and let her.

*I don't think this is funny.* He said that he wasn't known for his humor. *That's not what I meant and you know it. What do you mean, four babies? Surely someone would have known.... She would have been as big as a fucking house being pregnant with four babies.*

*Not nice, but I can see your point. Wendy isn't a small person; not fat, but she weighs a lot more than she looks. Maybe her body was able to hold it well.* Lauren told him to shut the fuck up. *No, I'm not kidding. There are women who can go through their entire pregnancy without even knowing it. Boyd told me of this woman who was in labor before she knew she was.*

*Bullshit.* He laughed. *This is.... Four? Are they sure?* He said that they were. *Are they sure that there aren't maybe a couple more lurking around? Just waiting to pop out at the last minute and make me even more terrified?*

*I'm sorry, love. If it makes you feel any better, I'm afraid too.* She said that it didn't. Both of them afraid was dangerous. *I guess you're right about that. But I can't help but be excited too.*

*I guess I am too. It's just going to take some.... Holy shit balls, Colin. Your parents are going to be ecstatic over this. You cannot tell them until I'm there. I want to see their faces.* He said that he'd wait. *Plan a dinner party or something. Invite them all over and we'll do it then. We'll say it's for me being home or some shit like that. I cannot wait to see your mom's face on this one. Four babies.* She was flipping out over just the two. *This might send her into shopping overload.*

Colin found out when she was coming home and what she wanted to do about a meal. Of course she left that up to him, but did request that Reese help with the desserts. If his new sister-in-law kept up her baking like she was, he'd have to get a gym membership. He was already feeling the pinch of overeating.

Another hour passed before he left the offices. He was a dad, or would be soon, to four children. Colin grabbed hold of the wall just as it hit him. Hard and between the eyes. He was going to be dad to four newborn babies. He looked at Devin

172

when he said his name.

"You drive here by yourself?" Colin nodded, trying to breathe around the knot in his throat. "Is there anyone I can call to come and get you? I don't have a car or I'd take you home."

He looked around as if someone from his family was going to suddenly appear. And when he saw Parker coming toward him, his arms loaded with something, Colin nearly leapt into his arms.

"Help me." Parker looked around, his body stiff now. "I just need for you to take me home. I don't think I can drive."

"All right." He sounded skeptical. Maybe he thought him insane. Colin was beginning to feel that way too. "You have your car? I just came here to get some roses for Reese when she wakes up. Mom sent me out of the house because she said I was hovering. I don't hover."

"You do. And yes, I have my car." Devin told him he'd see him in the morning when the paperwork was ready. "I just got some news that I can't share, so don't ask me. It's big, epic. But I can't tell you. I want to but I can't. So don't ask me."

Parker just stared at him for a full minute before just walking away. Colin walked behind him, careful not to get too close and want to tell him. He had to talk to someone and knew that Parker wouldn't tell, but he'd made a promise. As he watched his little brother, he noticed how stiff he was, how...well, he looked like he'd been crying. Before he could ask him about it, Parker turned on him. Not just to him but on him.

"You're fucking nuts; have you been told that today? Christ, the entire world does not revolve around you and your little secret. Perhaps I just don't care." Colin just growled at him. "Yeah, that's going to make me think you're less off your rocker."

When they were in the car, Parker turned to him again. Colin knew he was going to ask him, and he wasn't sure he could not tell him. He needed to tell someone or burst. But when Parker started crying, great gasping sounds, all his fear of being a dad flew out the window as he reached for his brother.

"I hurt her so badly. I thought for sure she was dead. Her body was so cold that I found myself looking for anything out there to wrap her up in." Colin held him as he poured out his nightmarish conversion of Reese. "I tried to tell my cat to back off, but he wouldn't fucking listen to me. And she just screamed and screamed until there wasn't anything left in her to do so."

"She's going to be fine." Parker nodded as he held on to him, his anguish over what had happened tearing him apart. "Mom said that her heartbeat is strong and that she's only resting. You know this, right?"

"But you weren't there. You didn't hear her screaming. I think for the rest of my life, I will never forget that. Never be able to forget how my cat hurt her." Colin looked at his brother when he pulled away. "I'm not going to let him out again. Not for any reason. He's been.... He hurt her, went against what I said to him and hurt our mate."

"Parker, you can't do that. You can't hold your cat within you or you'll suffer." Parker started the truck, his face set. "Parker, talk to me."

"I've made enough of a fool of myself, thanks." Colin told him he was glad to be here for him. "I'm fine now. I'll take you home if you're ready."

"I just talked to the attorney, that's why I needed a ride home." Parker nodded as he pulled into traffic. Colin had to

174

do something, had to bring his brother away from this line of thought. "We're not having twins. The mother is having four children. Lauren and I are taking them."

"They couldn't do better than to have parents like you two." It wasn't what he wanted from Parker. Colin wanted him to be shocked, scared for them, or at the very least, show more excitement than he was now. "I'm really sorry about before. I shouldn't have rained on your parade. I'm assuming that the rest of the family has to wait on the news."

"Yes. Lauren wants to be here when we tell them." Parker only nodded again. "We have to talk about what you said. You can't just cut off—"

"I'm a grown man. I know that I just disproved that to you with crying like a child, but I am a man and I can make decisions on my own. Believe it or not, I have been for some time." Colin told him he was worried. "Don't be. You should be more worried about college funds and the amount of diapers you're going to consume over the next three years."

They talked about nothing really on the way to Parker's house. Colin went in to talk to his mom and to see about Reese, but left without talking to his brother again. He would, he promised himself, but right now, he knew that Parker had his own things to deal with.

~~~

Reese wasn't sure what was wrong with her; every part of her body was humming. And when she turned to her back, she looked around the bedroom and saw Bea and Rich sitting at a little table…coloring?

"Confound it woman, this is not relaxing. It's the work of some deviant." Bea told him he wasn't supposed to stress about it. "Well I am. Who makes a pretty picture like this and just expects it to turn out well? Not me, that's for sure. Just look at this mess. Coloring a book at my age? It ain't right and you know it."

Bea leaned over her own booklet and stared at her husband's. When she just sighed and went back to her own drawing, Reese wondered how bad it was. Then Bea answered Rich without looking again.

"It's quite good, Rich. And you well know it. You've matched up your colors nicely and have a good eye for the way you shadowed the larger pieces." He huffed. "But you're working at it too hard. Just pick up a pencil and color it the way you want to, not how you think it is supposed to look. It's what I'm doing, and so does the rest of the world when they color to relax. Don't you remember how much fun it was when you were a kid?"

"No I do not. And I'm not saying that I've lost my memory, either. I'm just saying that it's not right to have pictures that are.... To your way of thinking, I can guess you've seen yourself some green zinnias and some…is that purple? Some purple grass. I'd not want to live in a world where the flowers look like someone had a mess on them." Bea looked at Rich as he continued. "You're doing it all wrong."

"You know what I like best about this picture? The very best?" He asked her if it was the bright blue stems on the flowers. "No. And I like my blue stems, thank you very much. I love this drawing and *my* art work because there isn't an old man in there being a fuddy duddy ass while I'm trying to relax. Now, I want you to pick up a color that you've ignored so far and shut up while you color it. I mean it Rich, you're taking away my buzz here that I'm having."

Rich huffed.

When Bea slammed her booklet closed and stood up, Reese was sure she was going to bash Rich over the head.

176

The elderly man must have known he'd gone too far when he stood up and pulled Bea into his arms and nuzzled at her neck. They were both laughing when they turned to look at her.

"There you are. Durn near thought you was that old man that slept his life away under the tree." Rich moved Bea's chair to the bed and then his own as he continued. "You feeling all right, love? We had to kick Parker out for a bit. He needed to freshen up with some air. He was afraid he'd hurt you badly."

"His cat." Bea nodded and helped her sit up. "He hurt me, his cat. He really hurt me. Parker was there too. He held me for a little while. Then I don't remember much after that."

"He converted you. His jaguar was a might hard on you. We're not sure what happened. Parker, he don't want to talk about it much. I think he was worried there for a bit that he killed you." She thought he had as well. "You're doing all right now. Can you feel her? She's right there."

"I don't think I want to know how you know that." Rich laughed and said he was just guessing. "What do I do to bring her to the surface or whatever it's called?"

"You think of her. Close your eyes and think of her right there." Reese looked at Parker as he leaned against the doorjamb, and asked him if he'd change with her. "No. I'm not going to. But I would love to see you as a cat."

She was confused by his refusal to change with her, shift she supposed it was called, but did as he said. Closing her eyes, she could see the big cat there, like she was waiting on something important. And when she stood up, stretching her body out so that Reese could see all of her, she felt something in her warm.

"She's beautiful." Her voice sounded rough, like she was hoarse. Then she remembered screaming in pain and thought

177

perhaps that was it. But when she opened her eyes, Parker wasn't standing where he had been, but at the doorway that led out onto their own decking.

"When you walk, be careful." She started to ask him why when she looked down at herself. She was a cat. Christ almighty, she was a cat with paws and everything. "You will need to get used to walking on four legs instead of two. It's not that hard, but something you have to get used to."

Walking on four legs was strange, but she managed to make her way to the door where he was. Reese didn't know where Bea and Rich had gone, but she was glad that she could share this moment with Parker. He'd given her this gift.

The sun felt good on her face. And as she stood up on the railing, she could feel muscles in her body that she'd never felt before. Her back was stronger, her legs burned with unused energy. As she leapt over the railing to the ground below her, she laughed when she landed on her feet.

*I guess it's true that cats always land on their feet, huh?* Parker didn't join her; he didn't even come out of the room all the way. *Come out and play with me. I'd like to see if you can find me this time.*

*No.* She was hurt by his rejection. Perhaps he didn't want her to be a cat or something. *You go on out and explore. I'll be on the lower deck when you return. Then we can talk.*

*Are you mad at me?* He shook his head but she thought he was. *Parker, I wanted this. To be a cat.*

*Yes, you did, and I'm really glad it turned out well. I was worried for a little while that he'd killed you. You have no idea how terrifying that was for me.* She watched him as he moved out on the deck now and looked down at her. *I'm not going to let him out to hurt anyone again. He hurt the woman that I thought he loved too. I won't allow him to do that again.*

178

Then he turned and entered their room. And when the doors closed to their bedroom, Reese sat there staring at them, wondering if he could really do that, not shift. She no longer wanted to run; she wanted to hunt him down and demand that he explain. But she had a feeling that she'd not get any answers from him, so she went to find someone that would answer her.

Lauren was gone, so she went to find someone else. Reese wondered what Boyd would do when she just showed up at his house. She only hoped no one tried to kill her as she was getting there.

# CHAPTER 13

Lauren watched her brother-in-law. Parker was sick. She wasn't sure what was wrong with him, but he was burning up with something. She wondered if it had anything to do with the fact that he wasn't giving his cat any free time. Hell, if she went for a few hours without stretching out as her cat, she was really pissy. More so than she was on her worst days. Then she looked over at Reese. That woman was pissed.

"Leave it alone." She looked over at Hawkins when he spoke to her quietly. "Just leave them alone. They'll get it worked out. I'm leaving in the morning, and I'd like there to be no blood shed on my last night home for a while."

"And what fucking fun would that be for me?" He just smiled and shook his head at her. "They're hurting each other. Even you with your thick head can see that."

"Yes, I see a lot more than you do. Parker is afraid of his cat." She said she knew that. "No, you think you know, but you can't. Parker and his cat aren't like the rest of us. We all shift, we all love becoming this other being. Even you do. But Parker and his cat are one."

"Explain it to me like I'm a green, shit eating kid." He looked at Parker then at her again. "I want to help them. And unless you give me good enough reason, other than that Zen shit you just did, then I'm going to make him shift."

"All right. Parker was ten when he shifted for the first time. We're not supposed to be able to do that, not at that age. He was so good at it that he could shift and return to himself in seconds. Again, at that age he shouldn't have had that much control over him." Lauren asked why he was able to and not the rest. "Don't know. None of us did, then or now. Parker would spend most of his day, and nights too, as his cat. Then as he got older, his cat would help him. That's why Parker can know when to plant and what. Which horses are going to be good for his ranch. He said that his cat tells him that."

"I don't understand. Are you saying that his cat has these special abilities? And what does that have to do with this?" Hawkins just stared at her. "You do remember that I'm armed, right, and that I don't like to be fucked with?"

"I remember. And what this has to do with this is Parker has a relationship with his cat that none of us have or ever will. They can talk to each other. And while we can figure out what our cats want, what they need, Parker and his talk." She looked at the younger man who was wiping his brow again. "He's trying to control, tame if you will, a beast that doesn't understand what he's done wrong."

"And what has he done that would warrant such a behavior?" When he didn't answer her, she looked at Hawkins again. "You know."

"No, on this one, I have no idea." She asked him if he'd asked. "Nope. I think Parker needs to figure this out on his own. On his terms, not ours."

"Bullshit." Hawkins laughed at her. "He's going to hurt himself holding this thing in. Look at him. He's burning up with what looks like a fever. Is that what happens when you try and hold your cat back?"

"I've never had to hold him back, so I have no idea. When I feel threatened or he feels he can handle it better, I let him." She asked him how many times he'd done that out in the field. "More than you want to know about."

Lauren tried to wrap her head around the fact that Parker felt his cat, which was a part of him, was responsible for changing his mate into a cat. She could understand that it was traumatic for him. When she and Colin had arrived at his home after the deed had been done, the man was frantic about the fact that he'd killed his mate. Then when he was calmer, almost too calm she'd told Colin later, they figured it was fine. Well, Parker wasn't.

"May I have a word with you?" She nodded to Josh when he spoke to her, just realizing that Hawkins had disappeared. "I have a request, and I think you'd be the one to talk to about it."

"Sure. But so you know, if it's dangerous or going to get either of us killed, then I have to talk to your parents. Good move, by the way, in getting them to adopt you. I might have suggested it myself if you hadn't." She was teasing him and she was pretty sure he knew it. The kid was smart and more street savvy than most adults she knew. "What can I try and do for you?"

"Doc Holliday is in town. The woman who says she's my mother is working with him to get either Dad or Mom to come to them so that they can control me. They will, if it means saving me, but I don't think that's their plan. To leave them alive after I go to them." She asked him if he was going. "If

183

they take them, I have little to no choice in the matter. Don't you think?"

"What I think is that someone should have killed them both long ago." He nodded. "I'm sorry, I know that she's your mom and all, but—"

"No. That woman is only the person who gave birth to me. The woman over there is my mom." She looked at Josh with new respect. The kid had it together, she'd give him that. "I need you to make sure that if they manage to get me, which I'm afraid they will, then you kill me."

"Why would I do a fool thing like that?" Before he could answer her, even if he had planned on it, she got it. "They'll use you. For whatever sick thing they have in their head, they'll turn you into the monster they think you are."

"Yes. And I'll have to do as they say. They'll make sure of it." Holding his parents was what he was saying. Or perhaps giving him the illusion of holding them. "You need to promise me, if they get me then you have to end this nightmare. Or have someone do it for you. Just so long as I can't be a part of their plans."

"It will kill me to have to do that to you, Josh. You have to know that." He nodded and looked at Parker and Reese. "They're hurting. Do you know why?"

"Yes. Dad thinks that he's failed Mom. Mom thinks that Dad hates her because she's a cat. They're not speaking, talking this out." Lauren asked him if there was anything she could do to help him fix this. "I don't think we can. I have an idea that if we interfere in their misunderstanding, it will only get worse. They have to have a fight, and once they do, it'll be fine."

"How so?" He turned and looked at her. "You have a plan for this too, don't you? Why you sly little shit. And here I was thinking you're about the best thing since flak jackets for women."

"Yes, but it's not really a plan so much as a hope." She nodded as he continued. "Stay out of it for now. I know that you can command him to do something he doesn't want to, but I think that would be a mistake. Not that you make that many of them, I'm sure but this would be huge."

"I don't make mistakes, you're right. But I think you might be right as well. I'm not saying you are, but you might be." He grinned at her. "This plan of action that you have, can I help you at least?"

"You already are."

She wondered what he meant when he got up and left her there. Whatever his plan was, she was sure that it was going to be better than hers. She would have just ordered Parker to shift, made him realize that he needed his cat more than he thought. But she'd wait. For now.

Lauren thought about the babies coming to her and Colin. She had been terrified out of her mind on what to do with just two of them. Having four was way out of her realm of knowing anything. She'd decided, after talking to Colin when she'd gotten home earlier, that she was going to raise her children like she did a squadron of men. With discipline and with rules. Lauren had an idea that she was full of shit, but she felt bettering knowing that something was in place. She and Colin had decided on something else too.

"We'll wait until we go and get them to tell the family what's going on." She asked him why they'd do that. "Because it will be a surprise."

"I think just announcing anytime that you're having four kids at once would surprise just about anyone. Why wait to spring it on them?" He got down on his knees in front of her and she held her breath. The man was just too sexy when he did shit like this. "Colin, you're not answering me."

"Because we can hold onto the secret for just us for a little while. Once the babies are here, we will have more help, more family around than we have ever had. I'm not saying that it won't be wonderful to have them here. But to just keep this part of our growing family for us would be nice. Mom will have a fit when they all find out, but it's for us, this time; it's for us to hold."

Lauren agreed. It would be chaotic and loud when the family found out. Just like they were on most things. But she and Colin, just an hour ago, had talked quietly about the babies. Picked out names on their own and made plans; not big ones, but plans that would shape the kids' lives.

One of their plans was to never dress them alike. They might have on shorts together or tee shirts, but they'd be different. Neither of them wanted to stifle their creativity by matching them to some insane clothing chart where they never got to be themselves. And they were going to be able to do what they pleased when it came to their education. Or the army route as she had gone. While they'd be there for them, advise them, they were going to try their best to raise them to be good humans, with a sense of what kinds of other people were around them.

Leaning back and watching her new large family, Lauren reached out to her best friends and asked for some help. Victoria and Tony were in town, she knew, and she told them both what was going on with this Doc guy and the mom.

*This witch, do you know what she looks like?* Tony asked her, then laughed. *Never mind, I see that it's her. The man she's with, he was at one time on my short list of people to replace some investors. Then I found out what sort of man he really is.*

*And what is that besides being a douche bag that is about to get the shit kicked out of him?* He told her what he'd found out. *So he's a gun runner and a drug dealer. That explains a lot about what we've been able to piece together. I need to find out what sort of shit they did to Josh before he was born. I think, and this might just be me thinking outside the box, that some of the drugs they gave Momma dearest were what made him such a threat to them, someone that they want to control. He can do some scary assed shit.*

*Victoria said to give her a moment. She's going to get something for you.* Lauren had no idea what she was doing, but she trusted these two more than she did most people. Excluding her family, of course. *Lauren, she said to come to her now. There is some next level shit about to go down, and she wants you here, along with Josh and his parents.*

When she stood up, everyone turned and looked at her. "We have to go now." No one moved. "Now, damn it. Not when you get your heads out of your asses."

They were loaded in the cars ten minutes later, and she looked at Bea when she smacked her on the arm. The two of them had grown very close, but Lauren knew that she hated her language.

"Next time a simple please and thank you would help." Lauren nodded. "Practice with me. Could you please load up and get going? Thank you."

"Or my way. Something is going to hit the fan right fucking now, and we need to be there to help out before some shit ball kills us all." Bea asked her if that was true. "Yes. Tony and Victoria are there now."

"Well, then. Let's load our shit up and get the fuck out of here."

Lauren was still standing there when someone honked the horn at her and asked if she was coming.

187

Bea was forever going to keep her on her toes, she just knew it.

~~~

Parker stretched his neck. Doc and Ariel were in the hotel across from him, and he was going to confront them. He glanced over at Reese when she stood beside him. They were going to go in when Lauren said it was all right.

"Are you ready for this?" She nodded; that's all she'd been doing for the last few days. It was time he said what he'd been trying to say for the last few days. "I'm so sorry that I hurt you."

"When?" He didn't answer her question until she looked up at him. "How did you hurt me, Parker? When you let me go off in the woods alone? When you rejected the idea that I had of us exploring the world I was new to together? Or when I had to go to Boyd about what was going on with my body, how my cat was going to change me?"

"I would have told you that." She just snorted at him. "I would have. I have a lot going on. And I never meant to hurt you with not going with you. But my cat hurt you."

"No more than I wanted him to. I told you I wanted to be converted, and you kept telling me later. Well, I think later was too long for your cat, and I'm glad he did it." He said he wasn't. "Too fucking bad. He did what you wouldn't. And had he stopped when you begged him to, without finishing the job, then I'd be dead. Or was that the plan?"

"No." He turned away from her only to have his face jerked around toward her. "I never meant for you to be hurt. You have no idea how it hurt me to know that my cat made you nearly die. That you screamed for me to save you and I couldn't."

"Well, you royally fucked that up, didn't you? I don't

mean with the cat changing me. I mean with your not telling me anything. And you did save me, both of you did. And for the years to come, if I don't murder your ass, we'll have all the fun in the world if you'd just get your head out of your ass." She turned away from him, stepped back from him. "When this is done, I'm going to go on runs. I have to do something, and sitting around the house, baking for the shop in town, is making me crazy."

Before he could beg her not to leave him, to tell her that she couldn't go without him, Lauren said it was time. Reese moved forward then, her steps hard on the road, like she was pounding out her anger on it. Josh was right behind her.

As soon as they got to the hotel, Parker ran to catch up with them. They were in the lobby when the couple they were there to confront came out of the elevator. No one moved for several seconds, long enough for Parker to see that Ariel was afraid while Doc, or Ryan, whatever he was going by, was thrilled.

"There you are. We were just coming out to see you. I think you might have something that belongs to us." Parker asked Ryan what that might be. "My project notes, for one thing. And this boy here. He is the property of Barker Benton Institute."

"People aren't property, Mr. Holliday. I don't know if you're aware of this or not, but I would think that would be a given." Ryan laughed at him. "You think this is funny? I don't. Josh here is our son. Reese and I have adopted him as our own. And we want you to butt the fuck out of our lives."

"Doc, this isn't going to work out like we planned. We should back off now. Come back to talk to them at a later time. Come on, we should leave now." Everyone looked at Ariel. "We have to go now. This was a mistake. I can see that now.

We'll make plans and come back at another time."

"Now wait a damned minute here. We're going to be rich off of this. You and I talked about this and we're taking this kid."

Ariel backed from them. Before Parker could figure out what was going on, he felt something hit him in the stomach, power like nothing he'd ever felt before. Just as he was going down, his body hurting, he felt his cat scream at him to hold on.

*You can't do this to me.* His cat told him that he had and he would. *I don't want you around me.*

*Too bad.* His cat moved round the couple, never taking his eyes off them as they moved. *You are hurting us both, and our mate, by doing this to us. Why can you not just let me help you?*

*You nearly killed our mate.* His cat told him that he had not. *You did. You made her hurt.*

*And you think it didn't hurt me to do that to her? Tell me, Parker, when she is hurt, do you think that she will think it a terrible thing that I did to her when she can heal quickly? Be stronger no matter what is done now to her? That if these fools do what they plan that she'll be upset that she can take them on better?* He told him he wasn't being fair. *Ah, but life is not fair, my friend. You of all people should know this by now.*

*I don't want you out.* His cat laughed at him. *This is wrong. You're going to get us killed.*

*Nay, I am not. Join me, Parker. Help me to save the woman we both love more than ourselves.* Parker looked through the eyes of his cat and saw it then. *He will kill her if we wait.*

The man, Ryan, had Reese. The gun to her head was hurting her, he could see that now. He looked at Josh and realized that he was scared stiff, not moving at all when he might have been helpful. But before he could tell him to get out of the way, the entire room lit up, heat poured over him, then nothing.

~~~

Parker opened his eyes and looked around the lobby of the hotel. Or what had been an entrance hallway. It was now soot covered, small flares of fire scattered around the room. Before he could sit up, someone pushed him back to the floor. He looked in the face of his dad and realized that he was speaking and he couldn't hear him.

Dad's mouth moved. Tears stained his face as Parker was held there. He wanted to tell his dad that he was all right, that he needed to get up, but every time he moved he'd be pushed back down. Finally, after several minutes, he could begin to hear slight noises.

"Just lay there." Parker looked around the room. "Parker, look at me son, not at the room. You hear me?"

"Yes. I hear you." He looked anyway, knowing that there was something that had upset his dad. "Where is Reese? She was here too."

"Over there. Your momma has her. She's just fine. A little sore I'm betting, but she's fine." He nodded, seeing his mom now. "I'm gonna let you up, but you don't move from here. I've had me enough scares for one day."

"Dad, where is Josh?" Parker sat up, his head spinning with the pain and something he couldn't put his finger on. "Dad?"

"He's gone." Parker felt his world come tumbling around him. "He just killed them all, all those people in this room, and himself too. He's gone, son. Just gone."

"No. No. No. He can't be gone." His dad sobbed then, tears rolling down his face in a steady stream. "He's here, just tell me where. I need to see him."

191

"That man and woman, they hurt Reese. He went after them and that woman, she zapped something at him. He just roared out like one of us and flew at her. Burning her and that other man to death." He asked him what other man. "Lauren said he was Henderson. And Holliday, he's hurt really bad too. They don't expect him to make it either."

Parker sat up and looked around the lobby of the hotel. Pockets of flame were still burning. He could see drapes were scorched. The staircase that had been so grand in this place was simply gone. The long counter that had been made of the prettiest mahogany was burnt as well, large patches of the finish peeled away from the exposed wood.

When he was able, he stood up. He looked at the floor tile, and it took him several minutes to figure out what he was seeing. It was a perfect outline of someone running. Next to it was another figure, this one with hands up and pointing toward where they had been standing. It nearly made him sick with the detail.

Parker walked over to Reese and helped her to stand. They held each other, not speaking but holding on to their love. When she looked up at him after several minutes, he could tell that she had heard too.

"He saved my life. That bullet, it was coming at me and he stepped in front of me." Parker was remembering more and more of what had happened. "Parker, I'm so sorry about this. You should have been told." He was confused, but he thought it was because she was still in pain.

"He loved you." Parker held her again, knowing that he could never get over this, never forget this day.

Parker had been sure that Ariel had figured out they were outnumbered. And when she turned from them, seemingly leaving them, Parker had dismissed her as a nonthreat. But the blast of heat that had hit him, the pain that went with it, had taken him down. She had killed him; Parker had been sure.

As he'd been falling, glimpsing what Josh had done, how he had morphed into a dragon so big had been a beautiful sight. And then Parker had lost consciousness. Now, his son was dead.

# CHAPTER 14

Reese was sitting on the blanket in the yard when she saw the big hawk fly over her. Yesterday had been a nightmare. But it was done. The bad guys were dead; the family was safe. Parker, however, was hurting. When the hawk landed on the blanket with her, she put out her hand to let him touch her.

"Are you going to him?" The shift from bird to boy was swift. "He's dying inside. Hurting in a way that isn't right. We should have told him."

"This is going to be all right. I promise you." Reese looked out over the paddock where Parker had gone early this morning. "I came here first to see if you were all right. And to tell you that I read the paper. Ryan is dead too."

"He died last night. From his injuries. I'm not sure I believe that, but Lauren told me to leave it alone. And Charles is dead as well. He hung himself in his cell early this morning. He left a note saying that after talking with his attorney, he felt it was better this way." Reese had wanted to ask if anyone had had anything to do with either death, but she wasn't really sure that she wanted to know. "I think you should go to him now."

"I will. But I wanted to tell you something. Victoria and Tony, they're going to let me stay with them for a few months. I will come back here from time to time." He grinned. "Okay, I'll be here every day, but only here, and not where people can see me. Not at first."

It was the plan. He was going to go away for a time then return. As the brother of Josh. It was going to work; Victoria had told her she'd take care of the few people that would question it, but it was going to work.

When he'd converted to his dragon, Victoria had come for Reese. Tony had grabbed up Parker when he'd been knocked unconscious so that he'd be out of harm's way as well. Once the room was cleared of all the bad guys, Josh had left, flying out of the burning building just as her and Parker were returned. It was the only way to keep him safe. The body of the boy had been brought in, and even though she'd never heard who had found him, Reese felt terrible that someone's child was missing still and no one would ever find him. Victoria assured her that he'd been alone in the world when he'd passed away; but still, she worried.

After Josh left her, she laid out on the blanket again. She was exhausted for some reason and closed her eyes to take a short nap. It was only ten in the morning and here she was napping again. Boyd had assured her that it was natural, after all the stress she'd been under lately, and to sleep when the need came over her. She was sure that even in a few weeks, she'd still be tired. The stress had been that much. Smiling, she let sleep take her.

~~~

Parker walked along the long lines of pumpkins. He'd forgotten about planting them, and now he had fat orange balls of them all over the field. Bending to pick one of them up, he was startled when a bird landed in front of him. He'd never seen a cockatoo, and was pretty sure that this was someone's pet.

"Hello, boy. Or are you a girl? I'm not any good at—" He fell back on his ass when Josh was suddenly in front of him. "What the fuck? You're dead."

"I'm supposed to be, yes. But as you can see, I'm all right." Parker was almost afraid to stand up and touch the boy. "Dad, I'm just fine. I had to fake my death in order to save us all."

"They told me you were dead. That you'd been…I never got the entire story on what had…You're not dead." Josh smiled at him. "Josh, is it you or am I having a stroke or something?"

"It's me. Let me help you stand." He put out his hand and Parker was reminded of the first time he'd done that, helped him to stand up. "I know that you're heavier than you look, but I can still help you."

The connection snapped into place again. Parker had felt lost when he'd not been able to feel Josh; knowing that he was gone from him forever had nearly killed him. Now he pulled the boy to him, hugging him tightly as he sobbed like a small child. His son was back.

He found that he couldn't let him go, didn't want to. As he held him to him, patting him on the back to make sure he was real, he thought of who might have done this. Who would have gone to such links to make sure that everyone, including him, thought his son was dead?

"Lauren." Josh nodded. "She's scary organized, have you noticed that? I'm glad…I wish someone would have…Reese knew."

"Yes. Lauren was afraid that if she didn't let her know that she'd do something heroic and try and save me. Grandma

197

knew as well; she had to know so that she and Grandda would be there for the two of you. Grandda didn't know, but he played his part better than we thought. I already went to see him. I hadn't realized he'd be taking it so hard."

"Yes. I thought when we went to the hospital after the… afterwards, that he was going to just curl up and die himself. I'm glad that you…Oh Josh, you're here." He hugged the kid to him again. "I can't tell you how much I love you."

He thought of all the things that had gone into making his son appear dead. All the things that needed to happen now that he was alive would be taken care of as well. Parker was sure that Lauren had that covered as well, how to bring him back into their lives without anyone knowing who he was. As they made their way to his truck, Parker hugged Josh again. His son was back.

They walked to the yard and he saw that his parents were with Reese on the porch now. His mom had brought out a tray of drinks, and what looked like a bowl of fruit. He had noticed that while Reese could bake anything, she didn't really eat that much of them.

Pulling her up from the rocker she was in, he kissed her. She'd done this. Given him a life, a son, and a home. Holding onto her, he fell back on his butt when his dad suddenly stood up.

"It's time." No one moved. "The babies, they're coming, and we have to go now. Colin just told me to go to the hospital. Hot dog and give me a bun, we're going to be grandparents again."

And just like that, Parker remembered what Colin had confessed to him that day and started laughing. His dad had no idea just how true that was.

# Now Available in the McCullough Jamboree Series

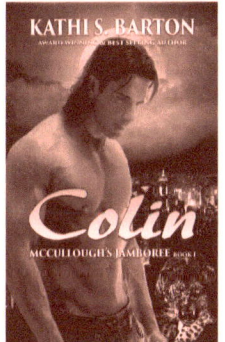

## Coming Soon

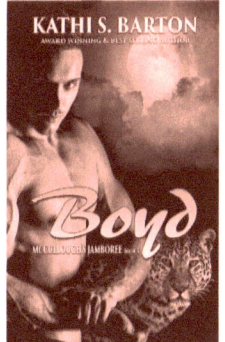

## Before You Go...

# HELP AN AUTHOR
## *write a review*
# THANK YOU!

Share your voice and help guide other readers to these wonderful books. Even if it's only a line or two your reviews help readers discover the author's books so they can continue creating stories that you'll love. Login to your favorite retailer and leave a review. Thank you.

AWARD WINNING, BESTSELLING AUTHOR

Kathi Barton, author of the bestselling series Force of Nature, lives in Nashport, Ohio with her husband Paul. In addition to writing full time Kathi likes to spend time with her eight grandkids, three children and three children-in-laws. She writes to relax and have fun.

Her muse, a cross between Jimmy Stewart and Hugh Jackman, brings them to life for her readers in a way that has them coming back time and again for more. Her favorite genre is paranormal romance with a great deal of spice. You can visit Kathi online and drop her an email if you'd like. She loves hearing from her fans. aaronskiss@gmail.com.

Follow Kathi on her blog: http://kathisbartonauthor.blogspot.com/

www.ingramcontent.com/pod-product-compliance
Lightning Source LLC
Chambersburg PA
CBHW032130170626
46808CB00006B/2178